MW01286909

A SAVAGE SPELL

The Nix Series - Book 4

SHANNON MAYER

HiJinks

Mayer, Shannon

A Savage Spell, The Nix Series, Book 4

ACKNOWLEDGMENTS

This series would not leave me be, but more than that the story took a direction that I didn't think was possible. I want to thank my editors (Angela, Tina and S.Page) and cover artist (JCaleb), for helping me bring Phoenix back to the page in a way that does her justice both in word and image. Thank you to my author friends who encourage me, my readers who love all my characters no matter how vicious ;) and of course to my family who loses me for hours on end as I dive into my worlds. You all make this journey possible. <3

PROLOGUE

SUMMER OF THE PURGE

"WHAT HAVE YOU GOT TODAY, ERNEST?" HIS BOSS asked him as the man slid in through the door, silent as a stalking jungle cat. The weight of the steel door that led into the aptly named "war room" should have made some noise, yet there hadn't been so much as a click for a warning. Which only set Ernest's rather human heart into high speed.

Ernest cleared his throat. "A new abnormal just came in, she is . . . we've been hunting a long time for her. We found her in a hospital in Montana. Childbirth complications. They alerted us immediately, as we'd requested."

"Name?" Gardreel asked softly, his voice a careful caress. Ernest knew Gardreel had been searching for one abnormal in particular and the idea that this could be her caused a reaction in his boss he wasn't sure he liked. His eyes glittered and the front of his pants tightened, his human body reacting strangely. The boss had just returned to the facility after heading a successful grab operation in Northern Ireland and Ernest did not want to upset him when his human body was already fatigued.

Ernest cleared his throat, again, and read from the single page on the clipboard he held.

"Name: Phoenix, aka, Nix.

"Age: Thirty-four.

"Abilities: Assassin. Knowledge of weaponry, hand-to-hand combat, tactical warfare. Considered extremely dangerous.

"Abnormal abilities: Unknown, but suspected ascendant. No training.

"Connections: Father—New York crime boss, Romano. Deceased. Dealt with demons.

"Spouse. Killian Fannin, leader of the Irish mob, abnormal. Whereabouts unknown.

"Son: Bear (Possible abnormal abilities connected to his mother's abilities.) Whereabouts unknown. Possibly deceased.

"Daughter: Un-named. Whereabouts unknown. Possibly deceased.

"Both children are off the radar, though being searched for actively.

"Medications prescribed: Patient can metabolize sedative at a rapid rate. It is suggested that all her meals be loaded with the highest dose of amobarbital possible. As we've seen in other patients, this will effectively depress her natural inclination to fight and increase her willingness to accept new memories." He paused. There wasn't much else on the chart. More would come later as they observed her, but she'd been in a perpetual state of sedation since they brought her in.

Gardreel looked at him over a pair of spectacles, his blue eyes sharp. "Ascendant? She is the one then, she has to be."

"I suppose," Ernest hedged, not sure he wanted to agree too much with his boss.

"Was she truly that difficult?" He tapped at the monitor they stood in front of. "She seems quiet. The redhead fought for weeks. In fact, all the other abnormals fought the sedatives far more. This one is, dare I say, peaceful."

Ernest stared at the screen with an image of the woman on the bed, her arms strapped down, her eyes closed, and her breathing slow as if she were sleeping. That would be the amobarbital keeping her quiet, yet his boss wasn't wrong. The other abnormals, when they were brought in, had fought as though their lives depended on being free, more like wild animals than anything even remotely human.

But his boss wasn't right either. She wasn't asleep, just lying there quietly if her breathing was any indication. Too fast for sleeping.

Other than her initial drive in with the medics, she'd been almost silent. Easy for anyone to deal with. A complete angel, if you asked any of them.

Ernest had heard from the other handlers of how an abnormal could fight when they were cornered. They looked human, but they fought with the strength of ten men. Some of them could even change their bodies to other forms. Animals or worse. Some didn't look human—though those were often destroyed as soon as they were located as there could be no fixing them. He shivered. Ernest had not seen any of *those*, and he didn't want to. Bad enough that he would have to live so close to these abnormals and their dark blood.

Of course, things had changed since Gardreel had developed the box and the incantation. Since then, their effectiveness at bringing in abnormals had more than quadrupled.

"Keep reading, what we have on her has been largely based on stories and theories. She's been here how long now?"

Ernest swallowed hard and traced the paper with a finger. "One week; she was brought in a day after you left. The doctor wanted to keep her quiet until we'd spoken with you and found out how you'd like to handle her rehabilitation."

If she could be rehabilitated. Ernest suppressed a shudder. If she could not be helped, she would be destroyed and that . . . bothered him. Death was a part of life here, but that did not mean he had to like it.

Gardreel stared at the screen. "Have they tested her blood? What is the breakdown?"

Ernest knew the answer, but he looked at the paper again anyway, struggling to understand how it could be accurate. "Fifty-five percent darkness. Twenty-six percent human. Nineteen percent . . . unknown."

Gardreel slowly turned to him. "That is the highest percentage of darkness we've found. She could very well be the key to this all. Her connection to the others . . . is it strong? Can she control them?"

Ernest shrugged, wondering why his boss didn't ask about the unknown blood. Wasn't that noteworthy? It was not for him, though, to decide anything. "We don't know yet. We would have to let her out into the general population to see how they react to her."

Gardreel twitched his long red coat, tugging on the lapels in a staccato pattern. "A puzzle then. The most dangerous of them all, yet she is quiet as a lamb."

Ernest swallowed and gave a slow nod. "Yes, she is a paradox indeed. The stories of her . . . they are there inside the other abnormals' minds as per their handlers and are all rather consistent with her violence and terror that she used against them. Yet, here she is." He waved a hand at the sedated woman with the midnight dark hair. She'd barely opened her eyes once, but he knew they were blue according to the charts.

"And you are the best at puzzles, aren't you?" Gardreel continued to stare at the visual of the Phoenix on the screen.

Ernest looked with him at her image. Unmoving. Harmless. Like a sleeping child with her hair spread across her pillow and those long, dark lashes fanned over her pale cheeks. She looked younger than her thirty-four years. Far younger for one with such terrible claims to her name.

Ernest had an urge to touch that soft cheek to see if it was as smooth as it looked. He swallowed hard again. Damn this mortal body and its weakness. He had to remind himself that she was a monster hiding under that beauty, that according to all reports, she was the most violent abnormal they'd ever captured, a dangerous, heartless killer who felt no remorse. If the records were right, she'd actively hunted the abnormals who'd crossed her father for years, acting as his enforcer. She'd helped make him the most powerful mob boss of New York. The others were afraid of her—according to their informant, she was known as the boogeyman of the underworld—both human and abnormal.

As if his thoughts had summoned their informant, the man appeared silently in the entrance to the small monitoring room.

"Do you have her?"

They both turned to look at him. This man was swarthy with soulless black eyes and an aura of otherness that made Ernest's skin crawl.

Gardreel chuckled. "Brother, do not be afraid. She is in hand and will soon be gentle as a lamb. Do you see her sleeping?" He pointed at the monitor. "She can no more hurt you than could I."

Ernest fought to keep his face motionless. He wasn't sure how comforted he would be if Gardreel had said that to him. But the informant was an abnormal. He did not know the boss, or what he was capable of—he had not seen Gardreel at his worst.

The abnormal folded his arms over his chest, flexing biceps that were easily the size of Ernest's head. A pair of overly sharp teeth peered out of his mouth, as if winking at Ernest, reminding him of what they could do should they find themselves on opposite ends of a situation.

"I've done my part. I helped you identify the abnormals you brought in. I helped you find others.

The ones who could've truly fought you are all immobilized in one of your facilities. Now, I want what you promised me. You give me back my life and pretend I never was an abnormal. And you keep her"—he pointed at the sleeping woman—"off me." Fear laced those last words.

This abnormal feared the Phoenix far more than he feared Gardreel and Ernest knew that was not smart.

Gardreel gave a slow nod. "Fair is fair. You have done this world a service. That is a reward in and of itself." He turned just his head toward Ernest. "Will you have George bring me around this one's payment?"

Ernest picked up the phone obediently and rang through to the head of security. "George, the boss is asking for you. Bring the box."

"The box?" The informant shook his head, wariness creeping into his feral eyes. "I didn't ask for no fucking box. I'll be taking my new papers, my money, and an escort out of this fucking place. As promised."

"It is just a manner of speaking," Gardreel said, once more twitching with his long coat, the ends fluttering around his ankles.

George did not dawdle, for once. He tapped on the door fewer than ten seconds later, and Ernest opened it, letting him into the confined space. Of course, he'd probably seen the informant arrive, and had been waiting with the box in hand. The captain of the guard took up what little room was left. Ernest found himself pushed up against the monitors. Or maybe he'd backed up, away from the abnormal and what he knew was coming.

"Why is the little one afraid?" the informant asked, although he didn't sound alarmed. Yet.

Gardreel smiled. "Ernest is always afraid. He is a natural coward."

George opened the box in his hands, pointing the opening at the informant. A dark green flash of light burst out of it, catching the abnormal square in the face. He went down snarling, shaking his head, but it was too late. The deep green magic coated his face, sank into his skin, and seeped into every orifice, cutting off any chance of escape.

The abnormal was on his knees, shaking his head, trying to throw it off, clawing at his own face. He was holding his breath. Ernest pushed back farther.

"It won't work," George said, bending to put the box on the floor and secure a pair of silvery bracelets on the abnormal. "Captain at the mountain facility said they got one like this. Best to kill him now." The abnormal gave a lazy lurch forward, and George pinned him to the ground with a big boot.

"Deal with him." Gardreel waved him away. "If you think we can use him—"

"Perhaps we can," Ernest said, his mind working through the puzzle that was the woman on the monitor. "Did he not say she was strong enough to kill one of his kind of abnormal? If in fact that is true, he would be an excellent litmus test for her strength and skill set."

Why was he saving the monster in front of him? The answer bothered Ernest, getting under his skin.

To see if he could save another monster who intrigued him with her soft skin and dark hair.

"You see, this is why I like you, Ernest," Gardreel said. "You may be a coward, but you are a thinking coward. Which makes you useful."

Ernest lowered his eyes, hating how little he felt next to his boss.

"Say thank you, Ernest."

"Thank you, Gardreel," he said. His shoulders shrunk as Gardreel slapped a hand on the back of his neck and squeezed just a little too hard.

"Perhaps you will make captain yet." Gardreel left the room, following George and the still struggling but mostly incapacitated abnormal.

The box remained on the floor. Wooden, with a lid that hung open, dangling, wisps of green magic trailing out of it. He knew the incantation by heart, although he could not himself produce anything so powerful. His abilities lay elsewhere. Not like the abnormals they were dealing with, of course—his abilities were a God-given gift meant to help humanity.

Yet, standing there, seeing the last bits of the spell dissipate and knowing the savage damage it wreaked on the minds of those it cleansed, he had a moment of doubt. Just one, yet it was enough to send his heart racing.

What if they were wrong?

1

CLEARVIEW REHABILITATION CENTER

ONE YEAR LATER

"Lucky you, Fi, you get to take the greenhorn around and hope he doesn't shit himself like the last one."

I smiled over my shoulder, tucking a stray strand of my dyed blond hair behind my ear. "As always, your jealousy rears its ugly face, Shane. Hard to compete with what's already stuck on your skin, but it manages."

The young guy beside me shook hard, bringing my eyes back to him, a tremor that was visible even with the straitjacket that pinned his hands down and kept him from flailing about.

"Ignore Shane," I said softly, keeping my voice even and smooth. "He's one of those who will never leave this place. Mind you, unlike some of the others, he can at least speak. Other than that, he's—"

"Crazy," the young man said. I looked him over, really seeing him for the first time. He was in his early twenties, maybe even late teens. Sandy blond hair and a face that made me think he could have been an actor in another place or time with the square jaw, light stubble, and perfect nose. Not a model, he wasn't pretty enough for that, but an actor for sure. The muscles in his neck flicked as he ground his teeth, which strengthened the hard line of his chin and the edge of danger that clung to him. No, not a model.

"Maybe crazy isn't quite the right word, but I'll leave it for now. It's your first day; I don't want to overwhelm you." I slid my arm through the gap in his bound arms so I could help him keep his balance as we walked the facility. This was standard procedure: show the newbies around, see how they reacted.

"You don't believe what they're telling me, do you? That abnormals aren't real? That it's all in our heads?" Blue eyes latched onto mine, demanding an answer. Begging me to side with him.

I shrugged. "You want to know what I think? What I really think?"

He nodded and lowered his voice. "I know who you are."

My eyebrows shot up. "Do you now?" Well, that was a surprise. I certainly didn't know him, and I hadn't thought anyone of his generation would have a clue about me. About who I had thought I was, at least. I wasn't that person.

No, you were never a killer. Never a monster. The voice that whispered to me was not my own, but it was familiar, nonetheless. It had been with me my whole time in this place, and while not exactly pleasant, there was nothing malicious about it. What felt like fingers tightened inside my skull, digging into my mind. I didn't fight the feeling, just breathed through it and tried to focus on the kid in front of me. Like a doctor digging out a sliver, it had to hurt if it was to heal.

The kid's sandy blond hair covered the top of his eyes as he nodded, and he spoke out of the side of his mouth as if he were a piss-poor ventriloquist.

"You're the Phoenix." He leaned in close to me, flexing his bicep. "You're going to break us all out of here, aren't you? I can help. I can."

I patted his arm and sighed. "You know, every person I've walked through the facility thinks they're going to break out and go back to their life before. Go back to a world that doesn't exist. We're all here for a reason, kid. The sooner you accept that, the better you'll do."

I guided him to a door, the metal panel cold

under my hand. The light above it flickered green, allowing us through. "Keep up, please."

His chest lifted with a deep, anticipatory breath. Like I *was* going to save him. What he didn't understand was that there was no saving any of us.

Unless you accept the truth. That you are not abnormal. That no one is. You have a disorder, a delusion of grandeur.

I nodded, knowing my handler could feel my movements as well as my thoughts.

"Where are we going?" The kid flexed his muscles against my arm over and over, digging his heels in a little as if he could slow us down.

"I'm showing you the facility. That was the main room, somewhere you can go once you've been deprogrammed." I swept a hand out in front of us. "This is the cafeteria. Some of us call it the chow station. Three meals a day and one snack before bed."

His heart rate tripped upward. I felt it pulse against the inside of my arm. Panic was setting in. It always did at some point. A woman strode toward us in scrubs, the same pale blue as mine. Her brilliantly red hair was swept back in an intricate braid that accentuated her lean face and bright green eyes.

"Esther, how's it going?" I asked.

"Fine as always, Fiona." She bobbed her head at

me as she passed, a smile on her lips that didn't come near to touching her eyes. Eyes that looked empty to me despite the dazzling color, which sparked a sadness I couldn't deny. "I'm headed to round up the crew from the sunroom. Meet me back here in fifteen?"

"Will do, just finishing up with . . ." I paused, waiting for his name.

He shook his head. "No, I'm not giving you my name if you're just going to change it."

"Who says we're going to change it?"

He jerked me toward him, impressive considering his current predicament. "Your name is the Phoenix. Not Fiona. And that's Easter. Not Esther. I know her. She worked for Mancini!"

Names from the past, names that likely were never real. I lifted a hand and patted him on the cheek. "You'll see, nothing is as we think, nothing is real but this place. Your name?"

He hunched his shoulders and I slid my arm from his jacket, turning him to face me. "Trust me when I say that you want to give me your name now, or others will get it from you in a far more unpleasant fashion."

Our eyes locked, and I tried to convey that this was stupid, that his name wasn't worth fighting over. But he was young, full of piss and vinegar, and he didn't understand what he was up against. He would, but today he still thought he could fight his way out of here.

He was wrong.

They'd all been wrong.

"I don't know what they did to you. I don't know how they even got us all here. But I'm fucking out of here!" He took a few steps back and a glow emanated from him, followed by a flash of light that forced me to turn my head and close my eyes as a power rippled outward that was less than human. His strait-jacket shredded, and I realized that whatever seda-tive they'd given him had worn off and he'd been hiding it well.

An alarm went off, the pounding of boots clat-tered across the linoleum, and a voice boomed over the PA system.

"EVERYONE DOWN."

I lowered myself to my belly and put my hands to the back of my head as the armed guards poured in around us.

Pressed my face to the cool of the floor as the young man screamed, as the sound of the Tasers going off filled my ears.

Closed my eyes as he fell to the ground with a thud that reverberated through my body.

Slowed my breathing as the smell of piss filled the air, competing with the smell of fear that rolled around us.

All of it happened in a matter of seconds. Twelve to be exact. The guards knew how to get a greenhorn locked down fast, always under fifteen seconds. They were punished if it took longer. I'd seen the trouble for being slow, once. Just once.

A tap on my shoulder and I opened my eyes. "You're good, Fiona. We'll take it from here."

I pushed slowly to my feet, contracting every muscle with purpose. "Thanks, George."

The head guard gave me a wink. "George the dragon slayer, isn't that what you called me?"

"George the dragon slayer," I said softly, a smile on my cold lips. "My favorite knight in shining armor."

I turned to watch as George and the other guards scooped up the young man. He was out cold, and the toes of his cowboy boots dragged across the floor as they removed him. My skin prickled a split second before Esther spoke to me, sneaking up on my right side.

"They always have to fight it, don't they?"

"I wish they wouldn't," I said, "but we all did."

"Who'd have thought you'd be such a softie underneath it all? Your story was the worst, but you're the good kid here. The teacher's pet." She laughed, but the laugh was forced. False.

I smiled. "Yeah, who'd have thought it?" I took a few steps, following the guards and the out-cold kid.

"You can let them do their job, Fiona," she called after me. "You don't have to help that kid."

I shrugged. "I'll be back in time for chow. Don't you wish I'd been around when you were going through your admittance?"

Her face faltered as if I'd slapped her. "Yeah, I do." She shook it off. "You'd better hurry after your new friend. I am not saving you any food!" Her forced laugh followed me, chasing me down the halls that led to the dormitories. We all had individual rooms lined up and down the same bright hall with too many lights and not enough air vents.

I didn't try to keep my steps light—sneaking up on the guards was not a good idea if you liked your face free of bruises. "George." I said his name long before I was within reach of a closed fist or a backhand.

George lifted his face guard as he turned toward me, standing at the opening to one of the previously empty rooms. Its occupant had died the day before. His body had been dragged out in front of me. I wasn't supposed to see it.

I can help you forget that sight. Do you want to forget?

I shook my head, but George didn't seem to notice or maybe he was used to me reacting to things he couldn't see or hear. Maybe he knew about the voice in my head.

"You think you can reach him? Calm him down like you do the others?" he asked.

The smell of urine wafted through the door as I drew close, competing with the industrial cleaner that had been used on the floor just that morning. "I want to try," I said. "He's young. I feel bad for him."

"Well, you've got until the doc shows up to sedate him," George said.

I slipped into the room, edging past him and the other guards. "Make sure the camera is recording. You don't want to get in trouble for that."

"Shit, I always forget. Thanks," George muttered, then snapped an order and sent one of the other guards off running to the control room.

I crouched beside the kid and scooped him up so his head was in my lap. I bent over him, my hair falling in a vivid blond wave that hid my mouth from being easily read by anyone, cameras or not. This was where it got tricky. The fingers I could always feel inside my head were there, but they were not paying attention. They were distracted. Not for long, but I had this moment and I used it to full effect.

"If you're awake, don't open your eyes. Squint them."

A soft squint followed.

"Listen to me and do exactly as I say if you ever want to see the light of day."

Another squint.

"Let them believe you are broken. Give them what they want."

His eyes opened then.

"Camera's on," George called out.

The fingers tightened as if they realized they had not seen something they should have.

"Do you understand?" I said softly, louder than before. "You need to let the doctors help you. They will help you."

The kid swallowed hard. "And what about you?"

"I'll be around." I forced a smile to my lips again. Something in me rolled, the part that had to stay hidden deep, far away from the surface. Like an undertow in the ocean, it swirled hard and dangerous under the surface of the calm water.

A leviathan that was not happy that it could not come to the surface.

"I'm your friend, kid. I need you to let me help you too. Think you can do that, Cowboy?"

He blinked up at me, fear thick in those blue eyes that hadn't seen enough years, that wouldn't see any more years if he didn't do exactly as I said. "Yeah. I can do that."

I slid him off my lap. The effects of the Tasers would take a bit to wear off, and there was nothing I could do for him right in that moment. He would have to wait. It wouldn't be long before he was given his own handler. Soon as the doctors gave him the clean bill, he'd be passed off.

Standing, I turned toward the door. George watched me, his eyes far too considering. "You talk to the doc lately?"

I shrugged. "No need. You want me to do a voluntary session?" I offered the words in a calm, neutral tone. Compliant.

George watched me for another beat, brown eyes unreadable in that almost too soft face. His gaze stayed on me long enough that the smallest trickle of sweat started down my spine. I worked to school any emotions, any errant thoughts. My own handler was still not fully focused on me; the difference was subtle, but there.

"Nah, you're one of the good ones, Fiona. I like that about you. You make my job easy." He gave me a wink and then waved his hand for me to leave the room.

"Good luck, Cowboy," I said over my shoulder. "Do what I said, and you'll be okay."

The kid's jaw flexed then softened and he lowered his eyes. "Yeah. Sure."

Damn it, he was already forgetting that the guards had taken him down in a matter of seconds. His ability couldn't protect him from Tasers specially calibrated to knock out our kind.

My handler was back online.

You aren't really an abnormal.

"Of course not," I murmured.

I stepped through the doorway, heading back to the chow station. As I got close, the clatter of dishes, murmur of voices, and smell of bland, barely seasoned food floated to me as the others ate their lunch. My stomach rolled, unhappy with the thought of the food available.

"You not hungry?" A guard at the edge of the hall touched his earpiece and gave me a look. "Stomach ain't happy?"

I nodded, used to the intrusion in my mind, used to them knowing exactly what I was feeling as my handler passed on information to the guards. "I'm going to lie down. Should be fine by dinner."

Across the hall, Esther stood from her table and waved me over. I shook my head and pointed back toward the dorms, motioning that I was going.

I had to have a moment of quiet, I had to . . . no. Not yet.

Breathing through my nose, I turned on my heel and headed back the way I'd come. All the way past Cowboy's room, from which I heard a muffled yell.

"Damn it, kid, don't fight them," I whispered, meaning every word. The soft approval of my handler washed over my mind, and I hurried my feet.

My doorway beckoned and I slid through, closing

the door behind me with a soft click. I stripped out of my pale blue pants and top, and sat in the center of the bed, folding my legs and closing my eyes.

I could feel the camera on me. I knew there were eyes on my skin, fingers in my mind, and it took all I had to hold myself together a few seconds more. Each breath came slower, softer, until everything was still inside me, the quiet on the surface of the river, barely moving, sluggish in summer's heat, giving the handler what he wanted. The quiet one.

The good one.

The obedient one.

The one who never caused any problems.

And then I dove through the surface and opened myself to the raging current beneath.

2

THERE WAS NO WORRY OF NOT BEING ABLE TO BREATHE under the raging waters of my mind. This was my quiet place. This was my escape from the guards and doctors. From the reality that was not real.

With the constant cameras on me and the fingers of my handler palpating my mind, this disappearing act of turning inward kept me from losing my fucking mind. Visiting this deep, quiet place gave me a chance to let my mind rest from the constant barrage of *think nothing, do as they want, you believe them, you trust them, this is where you need to be, think nothing, do as they want, you believe them, you trust them, this is where you need to be.*

I knew my body sat on the small bed in the small room, but another part of me stood amidst the frothing mouth of the river as it kissed the sea, then the water turned into an insubstantial gray fog I could walk through as if it were mist.

Here, my hair was black as night, not the dyed blond they told me was my natural color. I pulled the braid over my shoulder, like an anchor.

A scream cut through the dark of the fog, and I spun in shock.

This was a first. I'd wandered this strange darkness alone day after day, trying to figure shit out and memorize every possible detail about the facility. No one from the outside had ever shown up, which wasn't a surprise since the only other person I knew who could find me here was someone I would never, ever summon. My son . . . I would never risk him by trying to reach him from here. While I'd tried to find other prisoners who could meet me, it had never worked before. I wasn't sure the others could do it, for one, and it wasn't the sort of thing you could explain in a word or two.

A stolen word or two was all I ever got.

I knew my handler had his eyes on me.

I knew that I was watched more than any other inmate. They were waiting for me to make a mistake, or to give them something they could use. They were waiting for me to flex my proverbial muscles.

I'd seen how the other abnormals were killed, seen their lifeless bodies dragged out of their rooms after going to sleep. The handlers were the key. I was sure of it.

But I'd passed lie detector tests in my previous life, and I continued to do it now, though it was harder to fool the handlers.

Another bellow echoed through the dark space, and it deepened into a slurry of creative cursing that made me grin.

"You look like a fucking pig in a sausage skin three sizes too goddamn small!"

There was really no question about what I was doing. I sprinted in the direction of the thundering voice that belonged to the kid I'd just settled in his room. A shadowy figure lay on the floor, his cowboy boot kicking out at someone I couldn't see.

I watched until he went still, until he stopped yelling. He wasn't all the way *here*, though; the details of his body and clothes were blurred. Maybe it was a sort of semi-comatose state of mind.

Between us was another layer of fog, like a thin veil of material, gossamer and transparent enough that I was tempted.

Could I reach through it? What if I could bring him in here, with me, all the way?

Only thing I could do was try.

"Cowboy?" I called the moniker I'd given him to see if he could hear me.

His head turned, slowly, as if he couldn't believe what his ears were telling him.

Now or never.

I reached through that thin veil of fog and grabbed his hand. There was a moment where I thought my fingers would slide through his, that I would be the ghost to his reality. But then his body stiffened and his palm was hot against mine—skin to skin—and in that instant, I yanked him into the darkness with me. How the hell was this possible? What was different about him and me?

"Holy fucking prairie dogs." He stumbled onto his feet and into me as if I'd dragged him up out of a reverse limbo. His eyes were on mine, but they slid downward and then shot right back to my face.

I braced my arms against him and looked down, realizing the spectral version of me was still buck-naked.

"Get over it, kid. We have more problems than you getting a raging boner."

"I—" he stammered, his eyes closing and then opening but locking onto my face.

"Listen to me: I don't know how long we have here, or if it will ever happen again, so I need you to listen, hear me, and *do exactly what the fuck I say.*"

I kept my hands on his forearms. "Out there, you will call me Fiona. Here, you can call me by my real name. I *am* the Phoenix."

God, to say that out loud gave me a shiver. I was the Phoenix. I was the killer that every abnormal knew and feared. But in the facility, I was the good girl, the one who conformed more than anyone else. Because I knew that they knew who I was, and if I gave them one iota of a reason, they'd kill me.

And I wasn't ready to die.

He swallowed hard, and I tightened my hold on him.

"This place is designed to break you. They can see inside your head, so you have to do more than just say you believe them. You have to separate yourself from it. Give them what they want but hold a piece of yourself tight. Don't let them see it."

He stared into my eyes, blood trickling from his nose and mouth. "How?"

"If you're here, I'm guessing you have the same ability as I do on some level. Meditate. Find a way to be yourself here. I see a river, and I dive through the calm they see into the current below. That angry current is the real me." God, that sounded fucking hokey, but he nodded and didn't laugh.

"I can do that. Visualization. My mentor taught me that."

I didn't let go of him. "No one else in the facility has done this that I know of. Not even the people I knew from before."

"That was Easter, wasn't it?" he asked softly, and I

nodded. He blinked. "I'm sure I saw Snake too. He grew up not far from me." He frowned and shook his head. "How can this be happening?"

I didn't answer his question. "They are going to change your name. They call Easter Esther now, as if that would make her 'normal.'" I blew a breath out. "I don't know how to help them, Cowboy. But if you're here, then . . ."

"Then we aren't on our own." A light sparked in his blue eyes. "There could be others locked up in other places around the world."

My fingers convulsed, his words sending that current inside me into a maelstrom, even though I didn't move. "What did you say?"

He winced. "Well, I would think there are other places like this one. I mean . . . they've been gathering up abnormals at a pace that . . . it hasn't left many on the outside, and unless you've got several thousand abnormals here, this can't be all of us. I've been hiding the last ten months or so, picking up information where I could, but it was sketchy at best. What I heard made me stay put."

"Sweet Jesus," I whispered, slumping to my knees. He followed me to what made up ground in this place. "Are you sure?"

He nodded. "About six months ago there was another big purge after the first, a new law passed that abnormals are an abomination. They say we're causing humans to develop cancer, amongst a few other diseases."

I wasn't really surprised about that. The laws had been shifting for the last ten years, pushing abnormals into slums, out of the cities, out of schools and hospitals. What the normals—humans—didn't understand was that they were being controlled by the very ones they feared. I knew of at least three senators who were abnormals. One was in the running for the presidency by the way the polls had been a year before.

"I was taken before any law was put into play," I said. "Almost a year ago."

Looking at it through the lens of a war, I knew exactly what they'd done. A pre-purge of the strongest abnormals to stop us from banding together. We must have been watched for a long time before this happened. Years before, which made my skin crawl.

"Fuck, every gang in the world is headed by abnormals of fearsome power. None of them would go down easy," I said.

"They *didn't* go down easy," he said, closing his eyes. "They fought, but . . . they all fell."

Chills slid over my skin, raising it into bumps as I thought about those I loved outside of these walls. All of them abnormals. All of them powerhouses.

I forced out the next question, fearing and

wanting the answer in equal parts. "What about the Irish mafia? They were centered in New York."

"Gone," he whispered. "The big hitters were the first to go, before the purge six months ago, and the rest of us lost what little protection we got from them."

I bowed my head, my heart thumping as I heard his voice in my head, the Irish brogue soft and rolling through me. Not real, but my memories made it so in that moment, and I clung to it with everything I had in me so I didn't break and scatter to the four winds.

"Don't give up, lass. I won't be dead till you see me body."

Slowing my breathing, my mind picked up pace as I worked through what had to happen if we were to get out of here. All along I'd been thinking I just needed to hang on, that Killian would come for me if he could. With each day that passed, I knew the chances were slimming, but I'd not had an opportunity to make a breakout here. Until now.

I lifted my head and his eyes snapped upward, caught red-handed as it were. "What are your abilities?"

He swallowed hard. "Power surges, like an EMP pulse, but they leave me drained, and I have a knack with animals. That one I can do in my sleep, it never leaves me," he said.

Decent enough abilities, and the fact that I

couldn't smell him like I could smell an abnormal of a weaker ability was enough to recommend him to me. He was strong, even if he was young and inexperienced.

"They're going to put a blocker on you, something that stops you from using your abilities, and a tracer." I could feel him sliding out from under my hands, his body no doubt being prodded awake. It had happened to me more than once, yanked out of this place of safety before I was ready.

"We're going to break out, aren't we?" he whispered.

I gave him a quick nod. "Yes. But don't do anything until I say so. I'm going to try to get through to someone else." Someone I'd been working on for a long time. Someone who couldn't be taken down like most abnormals.

I let him go and he slid away from me, but his eyes dipped as he was wrenched out of the mist. A slow grin slid over his mouth. "You look good, Phoenix. Better than I'd ever thought a boogeyman could look."

Before I could tell him to keep his fucking eyes to himself, he was gone, back to his body, and that left me alone with my thoughts, the water swirling around me.

Back on my feet, not remembering standing, I paced the darkness and fog.

More facilities? How many? Cowboy was right about our numbers, far larger than the normal population would ever really know. So caging us all wasn't going to work. They would kill off the weaker ones, keep the ones they could use somehow. Especially if they were operating legally. The three abnormals in the Senate were influential and well-liked, which meant they were either dead or they'd failed to block this law. That was the only way this made sense.

"It can't be. I'm missing something."

I'd been in the facility a long time, almost a year, and I still didn't really understand what they wanted from us. There had been a few blood tests, some psych tests, and the constant probing of our minds, but no training. No cutting into our bodies.

Were we going to be killed off? That was possible. But if that were the case, why hadn't they done it yet? We were sitting ducks, and while a few of our kind had been killed, they'd kept the rest of us in stasis.

Were we going to be turned into some sort of abnormal army, weaponized to fight the normals' wars?

Also possible.

But neither option felt quite right.

There was something under it all, like the currents

I saw in my mind and they slid through my fingers just the same as the fog.

"Who the fuck is behind this all?" My voice echoed into the nothingness around me.

No one offered any answers, not that I'd expected one.

Although my father had been an enemy to other abnormals, that had been a power play to keep his side of the mob intact. And he was dead, gone.

According to what the kid had said, all the other big players in the underworld of our society were gone too. I would have no idea where to start on the outside, once I was out. Because I had to believe I would get out, or I'd lose what was left of my goddamn mind.

The faces I loved came to me, one, two, three, and I pushed them away, terrified that I wasn't completely safe, even in this place, and they'd be found because of me. I was almost certain that was how this was happening. That the handlers could see our very thoughts, and I suspected they were using them to track down our loved ones that were also abnormals.

I didn't think any of the other abnormals could feel the handlers, the fingers in their minds, the thoughts in someone else's voice, but I didn't dare ask. My son's face surfaced in my thoughts again, though, insistent, and this time I couldn't deny the pull to him. Dark hair and eyes like mine, his face was starting to look more and more like my brother and my father. Handsome, but it was hard to see those genetics become dominant. Not that he was anything like them. Or really even like me. Which was good. I blinked and . . .

Bear was right in front of me, on his knees, his hands on his face. Shoulders shaking, he sobbed, rocking in place. I'd seen him before in this place. Always in flashes. Laughing, smiling. Safe. And I'd always pushed him away to keep him safe. But never had I seen him like this. Not an extended vision of him.

It took everything I had to hold my tongue. I didn't know how safe this was, if he could be found this way. I dropped to my knees beside him. His clothing was torn, and blood trickled down one arm.

Someone had hurt him.

3

Rage curled through me, clarifying everything. I'd waited long enough, now was the time to move. My son needed me and that was all it took to solidify that I had to make the breakout now.

Killian, the man I'd loved, had let me down the night I'd been taken. While my memories of the night were more than a little jumbled and broken, I knew one thing for sure. He'd let me go without a fight. Part of me understood, yet it hurt me in a way I didn't like to admit. All that aside, I knew without a shadow of a doubt he would never let anything happen to Bear. He would have protected him with his own life before letting Bear be beaten. Which meant Killian had likely been taken into another facility.

And my son was on his own, fighting for his life in a world that wanted to destroy him.

"I'm coming, my boy. Hold on," I whispered, daring to touch his head, but my hand went through him as he disappeared.

Someone called my name and I looked upward, through the current to the surface of the water. Above me I could see my naked body sitting on the bed, eyes closed, hands resting on folded knees.

Easter (I refused to call her by her captive name when I was here in this place) tapped my physical leg. "Wake up, Fiona."

I blew out a breath and pushed off the bottom of the river, through the current and to the surface of the water, then through that as well, feeling the safety of my sanctuary slide off my skin.

I blinked once and stared up at Esther, fighting the thoughts that wanted to come with me. "Hey, what time is it?"

"Nearly dinner. You've been meditating this whole time?" She didn't arch an eyebrow, just looked at me.

Blank, she was blank. I smiled, forcing the same blankness into my eyes. "The doc said it's good for us to let our minds be empty. Don't you meditate?"

Her eyes didn't change. "I lie quiet on my bed and that is as close as I get. Is that what you mean?"

There was nothing for me to do but nod in agreement even though my stomach twisted with nausea again. The fingers in my mind were back, trying to soothe the anxiety that I couldn't still on my own. I pushed them away as carefully as I could. No need for alarm, just worried about the new kid.

You aren't the monster they say you are. You are good and kind.

She tugged on the end of her braided hair, twisting it around her fingers. "Do you want something to eat?"

I didn't but agreed to go with her. The food in the cafeteria was poor, though everyone else seemed to like it. The main dish was always the same, a type of gelatinous pudding that had a variety of vegetables splattered through it, and an undistinguishable meat on the side that was always overcooked with a faint bitter tang that I knew was the sedative. A barbiturate, no doubt.

Three times a day.

Every day.

I got most of it down, moving on autopilot, not letting my mind think.

Two cats wandered through the room, hopping up onto the tables, butting their heads against the people here. A few hands lifted, petting what were supposed to be therapy animals. The dogs slipped into the room next, tails down, eyes blank.

The leanest of the dogs sat at my feet. He was

light brown with dark points on his muzzle. A Belgian Malinois. His name was Abe and he was as trained as the dog that my handler told me wasn't real.

This was real.

This was the only Abe I knew.

I ignored him, though he reminded me so much of . . . no. There was nothing else. I ignored him. The other dog I fed was one that would be dead soon, I was sure. She was miserable, mean, and barely took food from me. Dead. Just like the other Abe.

"I should take food to the one downstairs," I said to Esther as I stood, thinking the thoughts they wanted me to. We needed to help those who fought the handlers understand that this was a good place. The animals were a kind touch, just not my thing. I didn't care about dogs.

There was no Abe in my past, no dog that I loved and who had fought at my side.

Esther didn't so much as look my way. "You do too much. You need to rest."

I paused. That was new. "I do what we're asked to do. To help the others."

Which wasn't incorrect. I took a deep breath, the sedative slowing my thoughts and my movements, and retrieved a second tray. The fingers in my mind loosened, same as they always did after I ate. I waited until they were gone from my mind, then I pushed back on the sedative's effects, clearing my thoughts at least a little. Like working through being tortured, there were ways to function while you were drugged, even if it wasn't easy.

There was a prisoner here, a man who fought the training and help.

A man who'd tried to escape sixteen times. Based on his rants, he'd nearly made it out the last time. I'd taken note of every route he'd tried, every trick he'd employed. Every reason they'd caught him.

Each time they brought him back, I thought they'd kill him, but it hadn't happened yet. I clamped down on my thoughts, just in case. I made my way to the stairs that would lead to the floor below us.

George was the guard at the door tonight.

"You on it?" he asked.

"All good. He has to eat if the docs are going to help him." I balanced the tray as George held the door open for me. Down the stairs I went, my bare feet slapping lightly on the concrete floor. The temperatures dipped the farther I went, and a breeze that shouldn't have existed picked up.

If I didn't take him food, he didn't eat. I was the only one he'd eat for. My hands tightened on the tray, shaking a little.

Everyone else was terrified of him.

Even the doctors.

The guards.

Everyone. So I had to pretend to be afraid of him too.

"Pete, you hungry?"

There was silence for half a beat and then he replied as he always did. "Fuck off, you fucking traitorous bitch!"

I sighed. "I'm here to help you, Pete. If you'd just listen to me, you wouldn't be kept down here. You could come up with the rest of us. You need to listen to my words."

The room was a simple rectangle shape, more long than wide, and his chains were attached at the very back of the room. No bars, no doors, because those chains were on each limb rubbing him raw over time. A rattle of chains and then he was right there in my face, straining toward me with his very sharp, very pointed, teeth bared. "Traitor! You were the best of us! You were the one who could have stopped this! You had a chance!"

I held the food out to him, staying just outside his reach of where his chains allowed him. I was being careful, that's what I told myself, but I put myself just an inch too close.

I locked eyes with him, willing him to listen to my words and understand how important they were. "Let me *help you*, Pete."

He snapped a hand out to the tray and his fingers touched my wrist. His eyes widened and he yanked me closer. I didn't fight, thinking that's what happened when the drugs were thick in your system.

Alarms didn't go off. The fingers in my mind didn't come back.

There were no cameras down here, not on a madman who lived and breathed in what would be his coffin one day at the rate he was going.

Pete rolled me around so my back was flush against his chest, tipped my head sideways, then bit into the crook of my neck, teeth sinking in around my collarbone. I closed my eyes and breathed through the pain and welcomed the darkness that washed over me, drawing the meditation into me in a blink.

Only this time, I took Pete with me. With his mouth locked on my neck, drinking me down, he had no choice as I dove below the surface of the river in my mind, taking his consciousness with me. A dangerous gambit, seeing as I didn't fully under-stand this ability myself. But desperate times called for daring . . .

As soon as we were through the raging currents and on the floor of the river, I jammed my fist back, unlocking him from my neck, then spun and fully pushed him off me. "You fucking moron!" I yelled. "Can you not see that I have been trying to reach you all this time? They have fingers in our goddamn minds! It's not like I could just walk up to you and tell you to bide your time. I am working on something!"

His jaw dropped open, my blood dripping from it. I glanced up at the scene through the river's surface to see him still latched onto my neck, his eyes closed, but there was no movement in his throat. We were in a holding pattern in the real world. But we wouldn't have long.

"Jesus, Phoenix! I thought—"

"I know what you thought, you dumbass. You fought so hard and what did they do to you? They locked you up tighter and tighter."

His jaw flopped open again. "And you . . . have barely a chain on you."

"Exactly. I did what they wanted, knowing our time would come. You can block them out, can't you?"

"Yes, it's why they can't compel me." He licked his lips and gave a little groan.

It had to be a Magelore trick. Blood drinkers, soul stealers, they were feared amongst abnormals for their myriad abilities and the power in their bite and gaze. Their ability to use mind control was well known. In the past, I'd wondered if the facility and the handlers were controlling us with Magelore magic, but I didn't know any strong enough to cause this level of destruction. Or smart enough, for that matter.

"You are the one person I can be straight with. There is a young abnormal here, brand new, and he can walk this place of darkness like I can. Our minds are safe from the handlers here and nowhere else. Can you meet us tonight? Do you think you can get your ass back here by yourself now that you've seen it?"

Pete nodded and looked around, a soft look in his dark eyes. "Yeah. You really think you can break us out?"

"Yes."

He closed his eyes and leaned his head back. "My wife is going to kill me when I get home. I went out for a meeting and . . ."

"Tonight. We meet tonight," I said and swam toward the surface of my mind, out of this place that was darkness and safety.

I cried out as I broke out of the river and opened my eyes to the real world. "George, help!"

A clatter of feet stomped down the stairs and Pete pushed me away. He slumped against the wall. "I'm sorry. I'll be good. I'll be good."

George yelled something at Pete, and we shared a quick gaze before I turned and hurried away. I kept my hand against my neck. The bite would heal fast, but the blood would show. I stripped off my shirt as I climbed the dark stairway, Pete's shouts echoing against the walls from below, chasing me upward.

I pressed my shirt against my neck, wiped it several times and checked the bite with my fingers. No more blood. I didn't want to get Pete into any more trouble than what George would give him. He hadn't meant to hurt me, and he wouldn't do it again. I was sure of it.

He was going to be okay now. I just had a feeling.

My handler all but purred his approval.

———

"What are you picking up off her?"

The voice was cultured, smooth like amaretto over ice. Almost sweet until you felt the afterburn reminding you that it could take you to dark places.

Three under-handlers straightened their backs, all at the same time. "She was attacked by the Magelore, boss."

"And?"

"She's worried about getting him into trouble," Ernest said. He'd not been in her mind during the attack, but he was not going to admit to that.

His boss rolled his shoulders as if easing a huge weight. "She has not broken from her desire to help people."

"No, she hasn't. Not once."

"Strange for such a monster to have a tender side. I wonder if we can use it to drive her to do as we wish?" The wide-shouldered Gardreel put his hands on the younger man's far narrower shoulders.

The younger man touched the nametag on his shirt. A human name. Ernest. A frown rippled what was otherwise an otherworldly beautiful face. His face was perfect, but that name was not and he hated it.

He cleared his throat. "You think perhaps she would help us find the rest now?"

"Not exactly," his boss said.

Ernest closed his eyes and flexed his fingers, feeling his way through the abnormal woman's mind. She was very strong, but the work they'd done had buried her powers deeply, lacing them up tightly. He doubted she'd ever be able to touch them again. Which was good, but it didn't fully solve the problem they were dealing with.

"She's back in her room," he said, and opened his eyes to see his boss staring down at him. "What would you like me to do?"

"She's done nothing wrong, but I have a feeling," his boss said. "She's . . . cagey. I don't believe she is fully broken."

Another of the techs—as the doctors called them —cleared her throat. "I could have Esther watch her." Her nametag said Susan. She hated her name too. But then, they all did. That was the thing about being trapped in this place. This human, filthy place. They were doing what they had to, but none of them liked it.

Susan ran her thumb across her fingers. "She'd be willing. They were friends before, but something happened, and Esther doesn't care for her now."

Esther had held out the longest of all the abnormals here. Fiona—or Phoenix as she'd once thought of herself—had broken first, the process so easy, they'd all been suspicious. But no one could hold out against the reprogramming for almost a year, not even a supposedly legendary abnormal like her. Even if she'd been playing them in the beginning, there was no way she could be now.

After spending so much time in Fiona's head, and a little in Esther's to give Susan a break here and there, Ernest was fairly sure he knew why Esther didn't like Fiona. They had fought side by side once, and he suspected that Esther had expected Fiona to help them all break out. That they would work together once again.

And Fiona was the first to bend to the handler's touch.

To Esther, that was a complete and utter betrayal.

He thought about sharing his beliefs with Gardreel, but it would not be welcome if he was not asked.

"You doubt my ability to hold her mind?" Ernest asked.

Susan's already pale skin went a shade whiter. "Of course not."

"I would know if she were being cagey," Ernest spoke to Gardreel. "She only ever thinks of others, and while that is not exactly our programming, there is nothing wrong with it. She is harmless. Like a kitten with its claws trimmed."

The boss didn't move, but the room went quiet and the tension climbed exponentially. "You think my impression of her is wrong? I have spent time in her head, as have you."

Now it was Ernest's turn to pale. "Of course not, Gardreel."

"Then watch her. Dig deeper, dig harder. We need to be sure she is broken so we can rebuild her to use as we see fit. The time is coming. The spell is nearly ready." The First Handler's sharp blue eyes swept over the three techs. There were more techs in other rooms, but too many together and the control of their subjects became . . . difficult.

Gardreel swept out of the room without another word and Ernest slumped a little in his chair. Susan leaned over. "I did not mean an offense, friend."

Ernest shook his head. "I know. He stresses me out."

She smiled and laughed. "You sound like a human."

"I feel like one sometimes." He rubbed a hand

over his face and closed his eyes. He needed a moment before he dove back into Fiona's head. Most of the handlers were given ten to twelve abnormals to watch, read, report back on, and *handle*.

But some of the abnormals required more oversight.

In this room were three handlers attached to the three most dangerous abnormals. Esther. Pete. Fiona.

Phoenix. He shuddered, a tremor running through him as he thought of her real name, seeing her as the bird of myth and legend, wings of fire, bright like the sun. To be burned to ash, only to rise from the flames and live again, stronger than before.

Another tremor caught him off guard as his skin rose in tiny bumps all along his arms. He rubbed his hands over them, trying to scare them away.

"You okay?" Jessica asked. As the third tech in the room, she had both the hardest, and strangely, the easiest job.

Magelores were impossible to break. But Jessica had wanted to try before Pete was euthanized. Such a nice word for what would ultimately happen to the abnormals too powerful to be controlled. Jessica was exempt from any repercussions if she couldn't reach the Magelore, and she got definite perks for trying the impossible.

If Ernest got it wrong with Fiona, he would not be so lucky.

He swallowed hard. "I'm glad he's not here all the time. He—"

"Stresses you out?" Susan offered, repeating back to him his own words, as if she'd just thought of it.

There was no answering smile from Ernest. "Yes."

Susan leaned over and tapped him on one shoulder, a touch of solidarity. "You are too invested in your case. Do you want to swap? Just for today? We are both capable of handling each other's charges."

Ernest looked at her, really seeing her. She was trying to be his friend. Something they were discouraged from having here. But he could use . . . a friend. "Yes. For tonight, let's swap."

He would have a break from the feeling like he was drowning in flames every time he touched Phoenix's—no, Fiona's—mind, and perhaps that feeling of stress would ease.

Perhaps he would be able to not think of her and wish that he could set the caged bird free.

4

No one came running after me as I stumbled up and out of the stairs that led down to where the Magelore was kept. The bite on my neck fizzled and stung, but the skin he'd torn with his teeth was already healing, smoothing over.

I ducked into my room and stashed the shirt under the bed. Not the best hiding place, but I didn't want to get Pete in trouble.

Not in trouble. I let those words run through my mind as I pulled on another shirt and headed out. I had to check on the others. See how they were.

Cowboy first, he would need a friend right now. He was probably scared.

I peeked into his room through the window in the door. He lay on his belly, arms sprawled out, the back of his shirt torn open. Welts ran over his skin in a perfect zigzag pattern, blood oozing from a few spots. But that wasn't what drew my eye, as much as I was sure he was hurting.

The back of his left pant leg was torn open up to his thigh, and his skin was visible there as well. A pinprick of blood blinked back at me. The same as all the newbies got when they came in. A tracer of some sort.

I hurried away, forcing all the questions from the front of my mind. He would sleep, and I would talk to him later about his stay here.

The brush of something against my skull stopped me mid-step. Like claws tracing up my spine and clamping down on my brain. The fingers in my mind had never felt like this before.

This was someone new and they were digging.

I swallowed hard and then kept moving as quickly as I could without running. Running wasn't allowed here. I would not run. I would not break the rules.

Through the mess hall and to the other side of the facility, I walked with a steady pace, thinking about the dogs that were kept here. Nice dogs. Therapy animals for the most part.

To keep us company and help us heal.

The fingers in my mind tightened suddenly, like long fingernails, and I stumbled against the wall, breathing hard as my vision blanked out for a moment.

What do you really think of the dogs?

The question was sharp and followed by pain that I struggled to think past. Like a migraine that came on in a bolt of bottled lightning.

"Nice dogs," I whispered. "Soothing. They are not my favorite, but they are good for the others."

The fingers eased their grip and I took a breath, sweat sliding down my face. I wiped a hand across my brow and picked up my pace again.

I passed a few other patients, nodded at them. Saw the blankness in their eyes.

What about the blankness?

Another bolt of lightning seared its way down my spine, emanating from the fingertips, and I arched against it, clawing at the wall for purchase as I struggled to form any sort of coherent thought.

A memory came to me. Esther had come in before me, but was still fighting mad when I'd arrived. I'd watched her then, watched her fight whatever had a hold on her. She'd arch back against the wall suddenly, balanced only on the heels of her feet and the back of her head. I'd hold her hand and try to calm her, not understanding.

How many times had I seen her hurt like that? Too many.

Too many times.

The currents beneath the calm waters inside of me spun faster, bubbling up, breaking through the surface of my mind. Whispering that darkness was the answer.

"No." I gritted my teeth against the surge of emotion.

Something tugged hard on my head, and I slammed my own skull into the sidewall.

Tell me your name.

"Fiona." I could give them anything they wanted.

The name of your dog?

"Abe. He wasn't real though."

He was from before. He was from before and he was gone, and I missed him and that was why I didn't get close to the dogs here. I didn't like the idea of losing another.

The fingers in my mind eased, apparently happy with that answer. I lifted a hand to my nose, touching the warmth that trickled from one nostril. I wiped it away and pushed off the wall. My head throbbed and I made my feet move in the direction of the dogs. They had to be fed, just like all the people had to be fed. I could do that.

I could feed the dogs.

And the current under the calm swept around faster and faster, tightening its hold on me. The fingers in my mind couldn't see it, but they would soon enough.

———

"She is broken, isn't she?" Ernest spoke quietly to Susan. Her eyes were closed, the orbs dancing under the lids faster and faster. She didn't respond to him. "Susan?"

"There is darkness in her. She hides it well, like Esther did. You are not hard enough on her. I think she has you fooled."

Ernest froze in his seat. "No, there is nothing like that in her."

"There is. I will show you."

He closed his eyes and dove into Esther's mind, subtle, careful. Their minds were fragile, and he didn't like how rough Susan and the others were. Gardreel had told him to be careful, so he was, he took his steps through his charge's mind as though it were a precious thing.

Esther's mind was . . . not like Phoenix's. Fiona's. He brushed through her thoughts as she ate. There was nothing to watch, nothing more than the drive to eat, maybe sleep, and a desire to move. But that desire to move slid away. He opened her mind carefully, watching her thoughts slide by. Until an errant one caught his attention. He reached out and took hold of the image that had popped into Esther's mind.

Her hands wrapped around Phoenix's throat,

squeezing the life out of her as her body bucked and her dark eyes closed.

"I'll fucking kill her!"

"Jesus." He opened his eyes and stared at Susan. She'd never said anything about this to the handler. He would know. He was the supervisor.

His jaw ticked. "Swap back, now."

Susan didn't open her eyes. He snapped his fingers in her face and her eyes popped open. "What?"

He took the token back from her, a silver angel wing hung off a leather thong, and he handed back Esther's token.

The gun had felt unnaturally heavy in his hand, and it shivered in a way a solid object shouldn't. But they'd stuffed it so it couldn't speak any longer. Thank God for that. He was glad to be rid of it. Made for killing and possessed by what could only be a demon, judging by the way it talked. Who in their right mind would want a weapon to *speak*, of all things?

Susan kept blinking at him as if she didn't quite grasp what was happening. Maybe because he'd never really spoken to her this way before. As if he were the boss. He stood. "I'm checking on her in person. And I'll be reporting you for not treading carefully in their minds. Esther is beyond shattered."

She gasped and her eyes filled with tears. "Please don't! The boss already hates me."

Ernest paused as he stood and stretched to his full height of four foot ten, a veritable giant among the three of them. "No, he doesn't hate you. He hates me."

He had no idea if that was true or not. He just needed her to stop crying. He wasn't good with tears. He didn't understand them.

With the token back in his hands, he reconnected quickly with Fiona. Her thoughts were solid, all about helping Peter and the new one, the cowboy. She wanted them to trust her.

How could Susan have not seen the truth that she truly wanted what was best for those around her? She'd never fought, and for that Susan wanted to punish her? Just like Susan had wanted to punish poor Esther. It made no sense to him.

Ernest paused and held out his hand to Susan. "Give me Esther's token back."

That vision he'd seen concerned him. He would hold both women's minds and keep them both safe.

Her jaw dropped. "Are you serious?"

"She is completely broken. We don't need you on her. The only thing left in her is a strange hatred of Fiona, which is completely unnecessary! I'm in charge here, remember?" Which he wasn't entirely sure of, he only knew that he had to take the gun away from her. Something in him whispered that he had to help Phoenix. She needed him.

"The boss told me to leave it." Susan bowed her head. "He said to let her keep hating Fiona, but to keep it in check."

Ernest shook his head. "That makes no sense. Why would he do that?"

Reluctance written in every move of her hands, Susan gave him the foul-mouthed gun. Whoever had thought of putting a soul into a weapon had one sick mind. No doubt it was an abnormal trick of the worst kind.

"I do not know," Susan said.

"Well, I am going to find out," Ernest said, his voice a sharper tone than he'd ever used.

He tucked the gun under his arm and headed for the door.

The door slid open and he stepped into the bright white hallway that was part of the techs' facilities. Sparse and smelling of disinfectant, the place was cold. He hated it.

Without a pause, he headed for the elevator that would take him to the lower levels where the patients were kept.

Human doctors bustled about in the upper hallway, taking notes on clipboards, and for the most part not even noticing him.

He was in the elevator and going down before he

could think better of it.

But after spending a year inside her head, he couldn't help but feel like he needed to see her in person, before . . . well, before the boss came back. Gardreel was going to do something. He was going to use her for something, and Ernest didn't want her hurt.

Was that why Gardreel had kept Esther's mind full of hatred toward Fiona?

As strange as it seemed, he thought of Fiona as a friend. Maybe his only friend. Almost as if she'd known he'd been there in her mind and had accepted him.

"Foolish, you are being foolish," he muttered to himself as the elevator trucked along, then coasted to a gentle stop at the bottom. They had to keep the abnormals tucked beneath the rest of the world for everyone's protection, but being this many levels down with them was unnerving. He swallowed hard, the door slid open, and he stepped out into the space.

Two guards turned toward him. "Short stack, what are you doing down here?" The guard on his left spoke with an accent that hinted of swamps and humidity, of voodoo and sweat-filled nights. Of demons. Ernest shook his head. Foolish.

"The boss asked me to check on two of the women," he said, once more pulling up to his tallest height.

The other guard grinned. He was newer, and there was a lecherous bend to his lips. "Check on them, hey?"

The first guard, George, leaned across and smacked the new one. "Never talk to them like that."

"You called him short stack!"

"I didn't imply he was going to fuck one of the inmates, dumbass," George said.

Ernest flushed red, because he hadn't realized that was what the other guard was implying.

"I won't be long. Ten or maybe fifteen minutes." He managed to get the words out without choking on them, but barely. Sex with an abnormal? That would be . . . an abomination of the highest order.

It struck him again that he was being foolish in coming down to this level. Why did he feel the need to check on her now, after all this time? Did he just want to see her in person before she was taken away? Or was part of him worried the boss had the truth of it—that he'd been duped and would pay the price?

Yes, that was the core of it. He was good at reading faces, but in person, not across a screen. He would look her in the eyes and see the truth of her soul, and that would be that.

He would see once and for all that Fiona was exactly as he thought she was, and not the monster Gardreel and the others believed.

5

THE INVISIBLE CLAWS DIGGING INTO MY SKULL dissipated into nothing. Was the other one back then? I waited to see if the ghostly sensation I'd been living with for the last year returned.

Like a breeze against my skin, the handler's fingers curled around my mind. Yes. He was back. I nodded to myself and picked up my pace. Slightly. Every instinct I had screamed at me to hurry, but I couldn't hurry. I had to be what they wanted me to be. And I needed help to do it. *His* help. If my handler only knew that I was a good one . . .

He would know if he looked into my eyes.

I nodded at another guard pacing the hall inter-section ahead of me but said nothing. They were used to me flitting about the areas we were allowed to roam.

The current of my emotions and who I really was boiled inside me, the waves getting larger, and I had to fight to keep the two sections of my mind separate. One quiet and calm for the handler, the other wild with apprehension.

Each passing second brought me closer to being found out, to being caught. Getting out of here would not be easy, but the moment was now. The Magelore, Peter, had shown me that. But maybe the three of us . . .

Sixteen attempts, *sixteen*, and he was in a hole in the ground so deep, I wasn't sure even I could get him out of it.

I gritted my teeth and fought to get my head back on straight. The handler was quiet again, not fully in my head which gave me a little breathing room. But that other person who'd been in my head—I was sure it was a woman—had only been in my head for a moment, but she'd cut through the walls I'd put up. What if I'd been with her from the beginning?

I stopped in my tracks, the realization hitting me like a baseball bat to the head. "I'd be like Easter if I'd been with her." Fuck, I'd slipped up and used her real name.

"I would never do that to you."

The voice was soft. I'd never heard it before with my ears, but I recognized it as surely as if he'd spoken to me every day. I turned and found myself looking at a man who barely stood above my belly button. He was just under five feet tall with completely white hair and the bluest eyes I'd ever seen. I'd even call them purple in a different light. Round face, round eyes, chubby body with limbs that seemed screwed on. Beautiful, though, like the beauty of a child untouched by the world.

Part of me wondered if I was seeing things. Part of me had thought my handler would look like a troll, a monster in the flesh who'd been willing to destroy a mind for their own purposes.

I wasn't sure how I felt about this beautiful child in front of me.

He pursed perfectly plump lips. "I've turned the cameras off. I'd like to speak to you."

I did a quick glance at the camera to my left, anchored above my head in the hall. No blinking red light. Hot damn, my call to him had worked.

"Why?"

"Because . . . I need to see if the others are right about you. Are you cagey? I see your thoughts every day and they are always about helping people. Keeping them from suffering. A noble cause, and you shine forth a noble light."

"A noble light?" I repeated the words back to him because I wasn't sure I'd heard him right. Was I asleep? Was this some sort of fever dream from all the sedatives in the food?

His pale face turned a light shade of green. "They're sedating you still?"

I tipped my head to the side and frowned. There was something under his arm that was . . . moving, wiggling. "Do you think that any of us would be trusted? Even with you in our heads? We are monsters to you, I know that. Do you trust me?"

He blinked and smiled up at me as if that would make what he said next okay. "Oh, not just me. There are many of us that helped to ease you through this transition. You, Peter, and Easter are special. Strong."

I blinked, not sure I'd heard him right. He'd said Easter, not Esther. Something akin to hope flared in my chest. Would he help me? I'd called him to me, but I hadn't been sure it would work.

The touch of his fingers in my mind was light, and he was only picking up what I wanted him to. This was better than I could have hoped.

"I would help you with anything. You are a good person." He smiled. "I would know. There is no darkness in you."

The thing under his arm squirmed and he put a hand on it, the black butt of it as familiar to me as my own skin. But I asked anyway. Shocked that he would bring it here, down to where the patients were. "What is that?"

"This? It's a token. It belongs to Easter. It helped us connect with her. To help her the way we helped you. I am taking over helping her. Susan has been far too cruel to her." He frowned and shook his head

I had never met anyone like him and his powers of mind control were beyond even that of a Magelore, but that didn't mean I couldn't beat him at his own game.

He touched something around his neck and I caught a flash of silver.

The wing that Bear gave you.

The thought was there and gone so fast I tried to block him from it, but my guard had dropped and he was quick. Far too quick.

"Who is Bear?" he asked softly, and those fingers in my mind tugged at the memories that wanted to surface. Not hard like the other one. There was no cruelty in him, and for that alone, I would let him . . . help.

I had no doubt he knew who Bear was, but he wanted me to talk. He wanted me to show him that I trusted him.

"Can we talk in my room? I feel exposed here," I said. It was a risk to trust him, but I had to do it. I needed a friend.

He smiled. "I am your friend. You can trust me. I turned the cameras off in your hallway and room, so we would have privacy."

He walked at my side, all the way to my room. I sat on my bed and he sat beside me and my thoughts were perfectly schooled. "I would like to meditate with you," I said softly.

"Of course, that is an excellent idea!" He beamed at me as if I'd told him I was about to blow him.

He closed his eyes. I kept mine open and spoke softly. "What is your name?"

"The name they gave me is Ernest, but that is not my real name." He gasped and pursed his lips as if he'd said something he wasn't supposed to.

"You can trust me," I parroted his words back at him and he relaxed, as did the fingers inside my skull.

"My real name is Eligor."

The thing under his arm squirmed again. Matte black steel.

"Eligor," I whispered his name and he shivered, his eyes fluttering open. "I know that name."

Damn it. I clamped down on my thoughts, keeping them to myself as a chill whispered down my spine. If his name was on point, then I knew what he was, but I would not say the word. Not out loud and not even in my mind. I'd faced his kind before, and I wasn't sure I was ready to do it again. Still, he was young. Maybe that meant he was malleable too. Maybe it meant I could use him.

I let a slow breath slide out. "I am very well read, you see, on certain subjects. I believe I know who you are. More importantly, I know *what* you are."

Slowly his eyes opened. I had leaned in close enough to kiss him, had I any desire to do so. Dark lines drew my eyes to his neck. I lifted a hand slowly and touched his left cheek, turning his face away from mine, baring his neck fully to me. The tail end of a tattoo peeked above the edge of his collar and then swept away, likely straight down his spine. The tip of it looked like feathers.

A tattoo matching my own.

"I have a mark like that," I said, my heart rate spiking to where even I couldn't control it. "Have you seen it?" Mine was a tattoo; I doubted his was, but that didn't mean I couldn't use the similarities to my benefit.

Eligor shook his head slowly, his eyes widening. "No. That can't be."

"Have you not seen me naked when I meditate?" Shocking if he hadn't looked. His cheeks flushed.

"I'm not like that. I don't look at you like that."

I breathed in, and with that breath, I tasted fear in the air. A smile slid over my face. "Eligor, I like you. I want to trust you. I realize that you could have destroyed my mind, like what happened to Easter." I waited for him to correct me on her name and when he didn't I went on. "By all accounts, I should hate you for holding me here. For watching my every move. For caging me. But I don't. I should, but I don't. Because you kept me from losing myself."

The waves inside of me crashed against the shore, demanding action, demanding that this was the time and the moment. I'd waited long enough and every instinct in me was rising to the surface.

"I can see your soul," he whispered.

That was interesting. "I don't think I have a soul, Eligor. Not with my past."

"Everyone has a soul." He frowned as if I'd said something to upset him. "Even abnormals."

I raised my eyebrows, his admission as shocking as anything else. "You don't want me to think my past is not my past any longer? You are saying that I am an abnormal?"

His jaw opened and he stuttered. "I didn't mean—"

"I won't tell." I smiled, the closest I'd come to a real smile in this place. "After all, who would believe me? I'm not supposed to believe I am anything but a crazy human who lost her mind to drugs and found herself locked up here for her own good, right?"

We sat there and he stared into my face as if he were trying to read a book in which all of the words were jumbled. Even though it didn't make any sense to him, he was trying. He was trying so hard to make me a better person than I was.

"And what do you see when you look at my soul?" I lifted my hand and cupped his face between my fingers and thumb.

"I see fire," he whispered. "You burn bright, your soul is like nothing I've ever touched before. Destruction and creation in one. It is . . . mesmerizing."

Tears filled those strange blue eyes and his whispered confession was all it took to break the last of the barrier. Words tumbled from him. "I don't like it here. I'm always afraid. They hurt the others. Like Easter. She was hurt so much, and I didn't know. I would have tried to stop them!" A cry slid out of him and I circled an arm around his shoulders.

The tide turned, and the power between us shifted. His thoughts no longer felt like fingers gripping my mind but like the wings of a bird. Frantic. Afraid. Alone. Bits and pieces of why he was afraid filtered through our connection, and it made me understand why he'd come to me now, of all times. I saw the boss he feared, who was more powerful than any of his kind I'd encountered before. And that was saying something.

I squeezed his shoulders tightly and took the leap into the abyss with a frail rope to hold me if I fell. "Are you going to help me escape?"

"How?" The question was asked with difficulty. "I can't even help myself."

"Let me guess, your boss is thinking of terminating me? That he doesn't trust me?"

He gasped and his eyes filled with tears. "Yes, I think so."

"And when they do that? You die as well?"

His lips trembled. "How do you know? How could you possibly know?"

I tightened my grip on him. "I know your name, Eligor. I know *what you are*. I have hunted your kind before, and I have killed them." I bit the words off as the current swept over the banks of the river, the rage rising.

"You're going to guide me out of this place," I said softly, pushing the intent into his mind, backward through our connection.

He nodded slowly and then faster as if it were his idea. "Yes. I can do that."

"You see, now that I know what you are, I understand how this works. I understand the ties that bind your kind and mine. You are going to help me get out of this shithole. And you are coming with me."

He would have the information I needed to find my boy.

His jaw flapped. "I'm . . . coming with you?"

I nodded. "Wait here. I'm going to gather two others and then we will go. It will be our best chance to work together."

He slowly nodded. "I can guide you if you get lost."

"Don't leave this room." I stood and he didn't move. I held a hand out and he put his hand in it as if we were making a pact. I grimaced. "Give her to me."

"Her? The gun?"

"She's mine; she was always mine."

"But she is bonded to Easter." The confusion in his voice was almost comical, but he handed her over to me. My gun. The gun I'd sent with Easter to help her on a journey into grave danger because we were friends and I'd wanted her to succeed. A loan, it had been a loan and these idiots thought Easter had bonded with the gun.

Dinah, bound up with the soul of my long-dead sister. She was a sidekick like no other.

"Hello, lovely," I said as the grip slid into my palm. She shivered but said nothing. I tipped her up and saw the wad of wax jammed into her barrel. "That blow out with the first shot?"

She shivered twice for yes, and I turned from Eligor. "Stay."

Things were about to get . . . messy. We were getting out of here one way or another. My mind was no longer bound with having to be careful. The plans I'd been running through whenever I meditated came fully alive.

I stepped out of my room and walked down the hall to Cowboy's room first. His door was unlocked and I pushed it open. He was still flat out on his face.

He would have to be last, then.

I paused, considering Easter.

She is broken beyond repair. You can't save her. Eligor's voice was soft but audible in my head. *It is forbidden to speak to our charges. We are not to bond with them even though our lives are twined and the fate of one becomes the fate of the other.*

"Well, that other one had no problem speaking to me and apparently neither do you." I turned away from Cowboy's room and strode toward the stairwell that would lead me down to Peter's lair. A few turns of the hall and I was there, approaching the guard. He smiled when he saw me, and I was glad it wasn't George. I would save him to the last to kill, and not because he was a nice guy. No, he was one of the worst.

"I'm going to check on him. I feel bad that I got him into trouble earlier." I kept my voice low and penitent.

"How you survived out there is beyond me," the guard said. He didn't have a nametag on, and he just waved me down the stairs. I hurried, skipping stairs where I could, all but running down them.

Be careful! Eligor's warning caught me off guard and I nearly fell.

"Shut up!" I snapped.

Sorry, you were running so fast! I wasn't sure you'd be okay!

"That you, George?" Peter called out. "I'm being good. Honest."

"I'm not. Keep it quiet, Dinah," I said as I lifted Dinah and sighted down the barrel of the gun. The chains that held Peter exploded on his left side as I squeezed off the first round, the boom muffled with her silencer. The thick steel door should've blocked any sound. The second round took the right and he was free except for a bit of chain dangling from each wrist.

"Fucking hell, you could have warned me!" he snapped.

"Can they see through your eyes?" I asked.

"Shit. Maybe." His eyes snapped shut.

Awesome. I grabbed his hand and dragged him up the stairs.

"What happened to meeting tonight?" he asked as he hurried after me, navigating the stairs easily even with his eyes closed. Of course, he was a creature of the night so that worked in his favor.

"A new player," I said.

"Who?"

We reached the top of the stairs and the guard turned toward me, his eyes widening as I lifted Dinah.

"Me," Dinah said as I squeezed the trigger. The bullet caught him between the eyes and dropped him backward like a tree falling. I bent and scooped up the key cards on the guard, the Taser, and a set of vehicle keys that looked promising.

"Never liked Chevrolet much, but it will do." I tossed them in my hand and then tucked them into my pants pocket.

"Dinah, nice to have you back," I said.

"Bitch, where the hell have you been, fucker?" she snapped, shivering in my hand as I led the way back to my room. "Seriously, I've had wax jammed in my barrel for a motherfucking year!"

"I didn't know you were here," I said, checking around a corner before tugging Peter after me.

No alarms had gone off yet, but it wouldn't be long.

Two more corners and we'd be back in my room.

I checked the next hall and jerked backward. "Fuck."

Oh . . . that felt good to say out loud.

"What?" Peter was right up against my back and he took a deep breath. "Shit, is that Easter?"

"Yes."

"Well, let's get her and get the fuck out of here!" Dinah said, thankfully quietly.

"It's not that simple. She's not Easter like before," I said. "They broke her." There was no time though, we had to get past her. "Smoke bombs left?"

"Yeah, I've got two," Dinah said.

"Do it."

Her inner workings clicked over, changing out her ammunition. That was the beauty of a soul-possessed gun—the usual rules didn't apply. I stepped out around the corner with Dinah raised. "Get down on the floor."

Easter turned to me, her green eyes wide. "What?"

"DOWN ON THE MOTHERFUCKING FLOOR!" I bellowed the words and the river in me crashed outward and upward, bringing with it all the darkness, all the death I'd survived and dealt out. The names of the lost were engraved on my heart, the ones I'd fought for and the ones who'd fought for me. I strode toward her and she dropped to the floor, but her eyes stayed on mine.

"I'll kill you," she said as calmly as if she were telling me she liked my outfit.

I pointed Dinah at her. "Change out, Dinah."

"Sweet baby Jesus. I don't want to shoot her," Dinah said. "She's my friend too."

"Not anymore she's not." I kept Dinah trained on Easter as we worked around her. A booming alarm went off. It had taken longer than I'd thought.

"Eyes open, Peter." I handed him the Taser, which he immediately jammed between Easter's shoulder blades. She didn't scream. That wasn't her style. A grunt, the click of her teeth, and that was it as her body convulsed and then slumped.

"Run," I said.

Peter leapt ahead of me, and I was right behind him. "Second door on your left. Grab the kid, he's not broken yet."

"This ain't a fucking rescue mission," Peter growled.

I pointed Dinah at him. "Incendiary."

"Oh, yeah, let's fry the Magelore. They're nothing but trouble," Dinah purred, shivering against my hand.

"Get him, Peter, or I'll leave you here." I smiled at him, meaning every word.

Peter snarled but slid into Cowboy's room. I opened the door to my room and waved for Eligor to join me. "Let's go, friend."

He stared up at me, strangely blue eyes blinking, horror filling them which made me want to laugh considering what he was. "You killed the guard. You . . . how did you keep the darkness from me? How did I not see the violence in you?"

"Later."

I took him by the hand and tugged him along with me as if he were a child. Peter stepped out of Cowboy's room with the kid over his shoulder and pointed at the kid's hip. "Why are we bringing him, exactly?"

I looked him straight in the eye. "Because we could be the last three abnormals with our minds still intact. And that kid there carries within him the equivalent of an EMP pulse."

"I'm carrying the bomb?" Peter lifted both dark brows high.

I winked. "You're carrying the motherfucking bomb."

6

Peter didn't argue with me after I shared that little gem about Cowboy. He just adjusted the kid on his shoulder and fell in behind me.

"This way," Eligor said softly, tugging my hand.

He didn't lead so much as direct me and let me lead. Which was fine. I could feel him in my head still, present but not trying to direct me like that other one had done. The alarm turned off as suddenly as it had started, leaving my ears ringing in the silence.

All of a minute and a half had passed. I knew we had another thirty seconds tops based on what I'd seen when the guards were to put down trouble. Under two minutes or they were in shit so deep, they were breathing it in.

"That's not good," Peter muttered.

I didn't disagree but said nothing. "Dinah, you ready?"

"Always," she growled, shivering in my hand. Eligor shivered too, but I doubted it was for the same reason. Bloodthirsty as Dinah was, she would be relishing this moment. Eligor was just scared.

I did a quick peek around the corner, seeing what I'd already known would be there. The elevator plus two guards, one of them George.

George spoke into the walkie-talkie attached to his shoulder. The other guard looked bored. As if the alarm meant nothing. This was weird.

I glanced at Eligor. "How far down are we?"

"Thirteen floors," he said.

I shared a look with Peter. The alarms had ended because they were waiting on the top floor for us with their Tasers and sedatives, no doubt. George wouldn't put up much of a fight; they'd let us through.

"There's another way out," Eligor said, picking up on my thoughts.

"Can we trust him?" Peter growled, adjusting Cowboy over his shoulder. The kid didn't so much as moan.

Tightening my hold on Eligor's fingers, I felt for him inside my head—and then followed that feeling back into his mind. He gasped. "That's not possible. You shouldn't be able to be in my head!"

"Heard that before," I said.

It only took him a moment to shut me out, but it was all the time I needed. Eligor was terrified of something here, and he wanted out. He wanted to flee, although he'd only just admitted it to himself.

"Yes, we trust him."

"We still need the elevator," the little man said.

I let his hand go, stepped around the corner, and lifted Dinah, all in the same smooth motion.

A squeeze of the trigger and George's friend went down in a crumpled mess. George's eyes shot to me.

"Fiona?"

I shook my head. "Phoenix."

His brows dipped. "This is ridiculous."

"We need him in order to get out," Eligor said.

If George had seemed perplexed before, it was nothing compared to the look on his face when he saw Eligor. "Ernest?"

Eligor cringed and Dinah snickered. "That's a shit name."

"Indeed. Regardless, we need his fingerprints and mine to activate the doors," Eligor said. "So he has to come with us."

I glanced at George, and the joint of his wrist. "We're already carrying one deadweight."

George shook his head. "You aren't that person."

I laughed, the first laugh in almost a year, and it

was rusty. "You don't know who I am, George. Not a fucking clue."

I grabbed his hand, yanked him close, and put Dinah's muzzle against his wrist. He didn't fight or even pull back, which gave me pause. I looked into his eyes and saw something there I didn't like.

Fervor. He believed in something else saving him, like a zealot.

I let him go. "Eligor. They know. They've known since you stepped off that elevator."

"Oh no," he whispered. "Then they are watching me too." He touched his head. "They cannot see now, but it is too late. They knew I meant to come to you, to speak with you."

George visibly relaxed. "They know, you're right about that."

My mind raced with this new info as a plan formed in fast-forward, an old plan that could be used again. "Peter, you remember that night at *Olive's Orgy* when I was still working for my father?"

Peter laughed, flashing all those teeth of his. "Yeah, I was there . . . shit, was that *you*?"

I gave a sharp nod. "Same move. Go get us some friends for a distraction."

He put Cowboy down, turned and ran back the way we'd come, his Taser in hand. He didn't need it, not with his abilities, but I took note that he hadn't used them.

I grabbed George's hand again, jammed Dinah's muzzle against his wrist, and squeezed the trigger.

The skin and bone exploded, and his hand came free of his arm. He screamed and fell backward, grasping at the stump of his arm, blood pouring from the wound. He'd be dead in no time.

Eligor gasped, gagged, and I held up George's still very warm fingers. "Thanks, George."

"You feel no remorse," Eligor whispered. "How can that be? You were always so thoughtful and—"

I turned my head toward him. "Eligor, let me be very clear with you." I paused as a bunch of the inmates were prodded forward by Peter. I directed them into the elevator as I spoke. "There is not much in this world that I care about, but my family tops the list. Right now, that is all that matters to me."

"I just don't understand how . . . how I didn't see this in you?" He stared at me like I'd sprouted a second head, which in a way I suppose I had. I was a person he'd never seen before. A monster that had risen from the depths of the currents that had hidden all that darkness.

I pushed the last of the inmates, patients, whatever they were, into the elevator. "Cameras in the elevator?"

"No, none."

I didn't believe that for a second. I shoved George into the elevator with them. His arm gushed blood, his mouth was open but there was no sound as he breathed what would likely be his last breaths. The inmates didn't so much as blink. These were some of the blanks.

I couldn't save them. Not yet. But they could help us.

"Eligor, can you untie some of their control? Let them be monsters again?"

Eligor was shaking hard. "Yes."

"Do it."

Using George's hand and Eligor's finger, I sent the elevator on its way. It would keep whoever was up top busy, but not for long. The inmates were shaking their heads as the doors closed.

"What's happening?" The slurred voice slid out of Cowboy and we all looked at him.

"Breakout," Dinah said.

I dropped George's hand to the floor, grabbed Eligor's, and took off down the hall toward where the therapy animals were kept. Peter scooped up Cowboy and followed easily. I didn't look back once. We had to move fast if we were getting out of here.

I had no doubt that if we were caught, we'd all be killed.

Thirteen floors was a long damn way to navigate when you were already made.

"What does that mean, already made?" Eligor puffed as we slid to a stop in front of the door to the therapy animals' room. A red light blinked over the door.

"Means they know, and are probably waiting for us at all exits," Cowboy said, wincing as Peter helped him stand. He took one look at the grinning Magelore and cringed, which only made Peter grin wider.

"Enemy of my enemy, people. Keep your shit together." I pushed the door open. We weren't allowed to go in any doors that weren't green lit.

This one was not green lit, but it also wasn't locked. A test of obedience for us and our handlers to see if they could keep us out.

Dogs in good-sized cages lined the lower part of the room, and cats in mid-sized cages lined the wall at eye level.

"What are you looking for?" Pete asked.

"Cowboy, you still got your connection to the animals?" I turned to the young abnormal.

"Yes."

I did a quick turn and pointed. "You got enough juice to bend them all to you?"

He nodded. "Temporarily."

"This isn't going to save us," Eligor whispered.

"You don't know her," Peter said. "Just shut up and let her work."

Other people might have been pleased with that

comment. Praise was supposed to make you feel good, wasn't it?

I started opening cages. "Pete, help me out here."

We hurried, flinging the cages open. The animals milled around us, and I glanced at Cowboy. He was sweating. Injured, he didn't have as much juice as he'd thought.

"Leave them all here to guard the room, have them attack anything that comes in." I opened the far back cage and the dog stepped out, eyeing me up. A definite stink-eye, even with Cowboy working on her. I reached out and slid my hand over the top of her head, feeling the rough skin there. She wasn't huge. A sleek gray female with scars all over her face and neck, half an ear missing, and one eye gone, maybe sixty pounds at her top weight. "This one comes with us."

"You've thought about that dog before," Eligor said. "You think she's special? Why?"

"Not the time." I snapped my fingers, and after staring at me for a long moment with that same stink-eye, the bitch fell in at my side as if she'd been trained her whole life. I didn't have time to answer Eligor's suppositions right then. But he wasn't wrong. I'd noticed this dog. And I'd known all along she was meant to be with me.

I led the way to the back of the room. "The

animals aren't brought in on the same elevator as people. They have their own way in and out."

"How do you know that?" Cowboy asked, limping along now on his own two legs, hand on the wall wherever he could. I kept a hand locked on Eligor as if he were a child, and I his mother.

"Because she's been watching, haven't you?" Peter breathed it out. "Jesus, how did you watch all this time and not lose your fucking mind?"

"Find the door." I deliberately didn't answer him because I wasn't sure myself and we were running out of time. I'd done enough hits to know when things were starting to get sticky, when the clock was ticking away, the noose tightening. However you wanted to look at it, we were in deep.

Because I had no doubt that at least three of us would be eliminated if we were caught. They might give Cowboy a second chance.

"There's no door," Peter said. "The room has no door."

"There's a door," I said calm as a summer day. "We just have to find it."

Dinah laughed. "You should ask the dogs where they came in."

I whipped around and looked at Cowboy. "Can you?"

He swallowed hard. "Maybe."

"Do it." We didn't have time for maybe. Bear

didn't scare easy, and I had no doubt that if he was afraid and alone then it was bad. Very, very bad.

Cowboy closed his eyes. The female next to me let out a low growl and turned to face the door we'd come in.

Peter did the same, his nostrils flaring. "They're here."

7

THE DOOR HANDLE JIGGLED ON THE ROOM I'D TRAPPED us in, a room full of animals that reeked with stress, shit, and cat spray. The cats began to yowl and the dogs took up a chorus that filled the room with more noise than I could handle after a year of near silence.

"Cowboy, hurry up!" I yelled over the din of animals losing their ever-loving minds.

Cowboy grimaced and took a step, then his eyes brightened. "In the floor!"

I didn't question him. If there was something in the floor, we were going for it. I dropped to my hands and knees, dragging Eligor with me. "Sweep with your hand. Look for some sort of pattern change."

He did as he was told. I'd give him that much.

Not to say I wasn't considering killing him once we were out of here.

I deliberately let that thought roll through me, but he didn't so much as flinch. "You staying out of my head now?"

"If they can still read me, I need to stay out of your mind." He didn't lift those strange blue-purple eyes from his task.

I scooted across the floor, my hands finding a track that I could just get my fingernails into. "Here."

Peter dropped next to me. "Good thing you got me." He dug overlong, thin fingernails under the edge of the lip and heaved the panel up, showing off a deep dark space.

A ramp led down, but no lights. I tugged in the dog and Eligor, then Cowboy next, and Peter last. He lowered the panel and we were plunged into complete darkness.

The sound of water dripping filled my ears, the howls and cries of the animals above us muffled with the closing of the door. "Peter, you're up."

"Make a chain," he said, "or I'll lose you."

I reached out and he took my hand, his skin cool. "Cowboy?"

"I got the short one's hand."

Peter tugged us away from the ramp, and then we were moving forward, quickly. The ground was flat and rose on a steady uphill grade.

Minutes passed. No pursuit came, but it would take them a while to figure out we'd found this tunnel. Maybe thirty minutes if we were lucky.

Thirty minutes.

"Cowboy, can you still feel the animals?"

"Most are dead," he said, a pain in his voice, a pain that I'd felt myself when my dogs had died. "I don't understand how they could be killed so fast."

"A gun," Dinah said. "A big one with a scatter spray."

I shook my head though no one could see the movement in the dark. "No, there were no gunshots."

"The boss could have done it," Eligor said. "He is the most powerful of us. I thought he'd left, which was why I felt safe coming to see you—"

"What are we going to do once we're out?" Peter said. "We all have trackers in our bodies, I'm sure of it."

"Agreed," I said. "More than one would be my guess. Kid here can do an EMP pulse, but I think that will be too obvious and they could reverse engineer where it came from."

Eligor was quiet a moment. "I don't know how many you have, but you are correct that you have them."

The female dog bumped against my leg, keeping

close. I wanted to run a hand over her head, to feel her there. But there was no letting go of my companions. Peter didn't slow, and he didn't take any turns. We kept moving on an incline, step after step. I wasn't surprised. The exit would need to be far enough away from the building itself so they were not connected, that there was no seeing one with the other. The time was ticking, and I knew we were on the short end of it.

"A hospital then, and an X-ray machine," I said. "We need to pinpoint all the tracers in us and take them out before we can do anything else. A scalpel should do it."

"There's a hospital in the facility," Eligor said. "With human doctors and nurses."

Peter gave a sharp laugh that echoed down the tunnel. I squeezed his hand hard enough to grind the bones against one another. "Quiet."

"Come on, Nix. I couldn't help it. Does he really think staying in this shithole is a good idea?"

Cowboy's breathing was labored. "How much further?"

"Hard to say," Peter said. "Thirteen stories down, on an angle… should be close now, I'm getting some fresh air."

Almost as he spoke, the light around us changed. Although still dark, there were now layers to the darkness, and even better . . . "Fresh air," I said. A year without it, and the smell had never been so welcome.

"Hurry." I pushed Peter and dragged the other two. We had to get the hell out of here.

Now.

There would be no other chance. I'd seen Bear for a reason, and Eligor had done what he'd done for a reason. Everything had aligned for us to make this one big push. We would not get another chance like this.

I felt it in my gut, every instinct driving me to action.

The ramp opened and we stepped out of the darkness completely. I did a quick turn, assessing where we were. A small bunker, a truck to the left, a road out to the right. For the first time, I let go of Eligor. I ran to the truck.

Locked.

I moved to the passenger side, checked that door. Locked as well. I lifted an elbow and smashed through the glass, then climbed through the opening and settled myself into the driver's seat. The dog got in beside me and woofed. As if she wanted to hurry me up too. There would be no keys in the truck waiting for us. I was sure of it, but I checked anyway. Nothing.

I bent down and ripped off the cover underneath the wheel and found the wires I was looking for.

Pete and Cowboy jumped into the cab of the truck. "Hurry, they're on us!"

I didn't lift my eyes from my task as I ran the wires across one another and the engine tried to roll over. "Shit, where's Eligor?"

"Just standing there," Cowboy said.

"We need him!" I snapped.

"No, we don't!" Peter snapped back.

The engine caught and turned over. I threw the truck into reverse and hit the gas pedal. Gravel and rocks spat out all around the truck as I spun it around, then jammed it into first gear. I leaned out the window. "Eligor!"

"Go," he said, not looking at me. "Go. They will track you through me."

I didn't need to be told twice. I hit the gas and released the clutch. The truck peeled out and we shot away from Eligor and the facility that had held us. I ran the truck until I was in the highest gear, moving as fast as I could.

"Jesus, slow down!" Cowboy yelped as I took a hard corner, the truck tires squealing against the hot asphalt.

"No." But even as I said it, it struck me that I probably shouldn't be driving. I could feel Eligor still, whether or not he realized it.

"Peter, take the wheel." I scooted out of the way and the Magelore did as I asked. My body started to shake, and I found myself watching through Eligor's eyes as the ones who had followed us swept out of the tunnels.

Eligor straightened his back even as he dropped to his knees.

But his eyes, and subsequently mine, were locked on the main figure that strode out of the cave. He was taller than every other person present, mostly humans to be fair, and his dark red cloak swirled out around him on a breeze that I couldn't feel, a breeze that stirred nothing else.

"What are you seeing?" Cowboy asked.

"Shh." I absently slapped a hand over his mouth.

Eligor didn't look away from that man.

That is the boss. He is dangerous. He will come for you, Phoenix. I . . . am sorry for my part in this. He would have found you for sure if I'd stayed with you.

"Eligor, run," I said. "Fight, do something!"

I am doing something. You know what I am, so you know what he is, and what he is capable of. I thought . . . that he was right about the abnormals. We have no other tokens of yours, so we will not be able to connect to your mind again. And I am going to cut you off. He touched his pocket and I found my hand moving to my own pocket. I pulled the silver wing that Bear had given me there. He'd slipped them in at some point.

The boss stepped toward him. Long, white, curling locks flowed over his shoulders, and eyes the same blue-purple as Eligor's stared down at the much smaller man. "Ernest, what have you been up to? Did you fall in love with our captive?"

"No," Eligor said, but the denial fell flat even to me. Even now, after what he'd seen me do, he thought I was worth saving.

That I wasn't the evil monster I'd been made out to be. That I was meant for more than the facility would do to me.

I gripped the dash of the truck.

Dinah trembled as she no doubt picked up on my emotions. "Do we need to go back?" she asked.

I shook my head. "No, but I need to see how they overpower him. It will help us."

"Smart," Dinah said. "You were always too smart for your own good."

The boss stepped up to Eligor, reached out and touched the miniscule man in the middle of the forehead, then drew his finger back with a twist. Something sticky and long went with him. Like glowing spiderweb. I could guess at what it was. Or who it was. The essence of Eligor.

His last thought was simple. *He has all that I am now. Do not trust me.*

"Eligor?"

Nothing. Either he was dead and what was left of

him was wrapped up in that web shit, or he really had cut me off. Either way, we weren't going to get more help from him. I blinked and rubbed at my eyes as I came back to the present.

"So . . ." Cowboy leaned around the dog who'd plopped herself in between us. "Any idea where we are?"

I shook my head. "We drive until we find something. And then we drive until we hit a hospital. If we can't use your EMP pulse, then we need something else to derail the tracers."

And then I was going to find my family. But in order to get to them, I would have to navigate the new laws about abnormals. Which meant I needed to learn why we were being targeted.

"Dinah," I touched her handle, "how was Easter taken?"

"She was sleeping," Dinah said. "She'd eaten at a place, a restaurant in London—"

Peter cut her off. "I was nowhere near London. I was coming back from a job in Montreal. Pulled off the side of the road to sleep."

Cowboy nodded. "I was sleeping too when they took me. Like I said, I'd been out on the range for almost the whole year, keeping myself hidden. That week before I was caught me and my boss, we'd been driving cattle for a week and finally had a break back at the ranch. Texas, to be exact."

They both looked at me. "I was in Montana." They didn't need to know why I'd been in the hospital. I'd spent the last year forcing those memories down deep to protect my loved ones. Because even if I had never fully understood what the facility wanted from us, I'd known they would use every tool at their disposal to force us into line.

Including hurting those we loved.

Trapping them.

Torturing them.

An image of my son, the one I'd seen in the darkness, danced through my mind. It struck me that he must have been chasing something. I could see that now in the way his knees had been splayed on the ground.

"I heard that you and that Irish bastard Fannin took up together," Peter said. "Were you with him when you were taken?"

My jaw ticked and my heart hurt at the thought of Killian. Of how he'd let me down. I didn't think he'd betrayed me; he wasn't that man. But he'd let me go so easily. It *felt* like a betrayal.

Twice. I'd been fooled twice by men that I'd stupidly given my heart to.

"Yes, he was there when I was taken," I said.

"Fuck, then they got you both." Peter shook his head.

I mimicked him, shaking my head. "No, they

didn't get him." And this was the part that hurt, the rage and betrayal I'd had to stuff down into the currents of the river inside my mind to keep from doing as Peter had done, flinging myself at every opportunity to escape. "He let them take me."

8

WE DROVE FOR NEARLY TWO HOURS WITH NO MORE than a handful of words exchanged between us.

It seemed that my little bombshell that Killian had allowed me to be taken was enough to keep the two men quiet. Peter at least knew of Killian, how in the abnormal world, he was known for his sense of justice, and his willingness to fight for those who weren't strong enough to fight for themselves.

It was one of the things I loved about him, and the thing that hurt the most about him just letting me go without a fight.

"I'm not going back there," Peter said as we finally found a road with a sign pointing to the interstate.

"You want me to kill you?" Dinah asked. "If the time comes?"

He didn't hesitate. "Yes."

"Me too," Cowboy said.

Dinah grumbled. "Damn it, and who gets to kill me? Huh? Nobody ever thinks about the gun's feelings on this topic, do they?"

I laid a hand over her. "Do like Eleanor."

I'd had two guns at one point. Dinah and Eleanor. Eleanor had held the soul of my mother, and when she'd been forced to shoot at me, she'd deliberately backfired, killing herself instead of me.

A sigh grumbled out of her. "My point is that no one in the last year has so much as wiggled my trigger."

"You've *misfired* before." I put heavy emphasis on that one word. Dinah was not supposed to be able to shoot without having someone pull her trigger, but she was, for lack of a better explanation, trigger happy. She'd shot on her own enough times that I knew she could.

Another grumble, but she went quiet after that.

The clock on the dashboard said 10:01 p.m. There was no radio.

"There." Cowboy pointed at a sign as we came up to it. A hospital was a few miles away. "What do you think the chances are we can get in and out?"

I looked at him and shrugged. "Not bad."

"Liar." Peter laughed.

The silver-gray dog lifted her head to stare at the

Magelore and let out a low grumble. I put a hand on her head, and she calmed immediately.

Cowboy cleared his throat. "I've tied her to you. She's not trained, but she'll always understand your commands. And she'll always come back to you. Even if something happens to me. She's your dog now, through and through."

I nodded. "Any idea on her breed?"

"Cane Corso, and pit bull, I think," he said, running a hand over her head. "She was used in dog-fighting matches. She's tough and has more than a little bit of a mean streak in her."

Peter barked a laugh. "A fitting pair."

I'd already surmised that much from the little I'd seen of her while I was down there. No one had been able to get close to her, and I wasn't sure why they'd kept her. She sure as shit wasn't a therapy dog. Then again, she hadn't been there long.

"They fed the bad ones to me," Peter said. "She can smell that I'm a predator. That's why she don't like me. That mush you brought me was bullshit, but they never told you that, did they?"

Now it was my turn to laugh. "I knew what they fed you when I didn't. The only reason I brought you that fucking mush was me trying to get through your thick skull to make you see we could work together."

I lifted a hand and touched the bite on my neck. It had healed, but I would always have a weakness for him now, for believing him. That was the way a Magelore worked, manipulating everyone around them.

"You really married?" I asked.

He nodded. "Yes. Though I've no idea if she'd still be waiting. Human, not abnormal." He shot a look at me. "Some of them have a thing for abnormals, turns them on."

I didn't care about that. "Don't call her. Don't think about going to her. Not yet. We don't know how tied your handler is to you still."

"I'm not a fucking moron," he growled. But I heard the defense in his voice. I looked at Cowboy.

"Same for you. No phones, no nothing. Not even your mother can know you are out."

"No one for me to call," Cowboy said flatly. "Family is all gone 'cept for a cousin that now I'm thinking might have got a payday for handing me over."

I stared out the front window and twisted the rearview mirror so I could check it every few minutes. Lights came into view and we were suddenly on the interstate with other cars around us.

"Two more exits, then the hospital," Peter said.

"Hurry," I said, rubbing at my neck. "They're on us already."

"Shit, can you see them?" Cowboy twisted around in his seat to look.

"No. But they are. I can . . . feel them."

They both looked at me, but neither questioned me. Because as weird as that sounded, it was our world. And I wasn't lying. There was a sense of being hunted that you only knew if you'd been hunted repeatedly. The tracers were already doing their job, almost humming under my skin, only for me it was everywhere. The hum was everywhere.

Peter took the exit we needed and drove quickly through a series of suburbs before the hospital came into view.

"Carlisle Hospital," Cowboy said. "Doesn't actually say where we are."

I snorted. "You didn't look at the license plates on the cars? We're in Pennsylvania."

Which was good, not too far from New York in the scope of things. I needed answers, and I was going to get them one way or another. I'd start at Killian's bar in New York to see if there was any clue as to where he'd taken Bear.

Peter pulled into a parking lot and we filed out. "Leave the windows down," I said, and looked at the dog. She needed a name.

"Wait. Guard," I said, and she sat and gave me a look that said it all. She thought it was foolish but would do as she was told. I smiled and tucked Dinah into the waistband of my loose uniform pants. At least the crappy clothes would help me blend in with the hospital staff. Same with Peter. Cowboy, on the other hand, looked like shit, his pants and shirt ripped and his wounds obvious.

"Follow me." I pulled Cowboy toward me, sliding his arm over my neck and mine around his waist. He startled a little but settled into letting me help him.

"You know where you're going?" Peter asked.

I didn't bother to answer him, and Dinah snickered. "He asks as if you've been here before. Shut up, Magelore, and follow the boss lady."

"She always this mouthy?" he muttered.

I smiled, and even if it was tight, it was at least real. "She's been nice, so far."

The doors to Carlisle Hospital slid open and we walked through. It was a big hospital, which would work in our favor. The staff in a smaller place would notice visitors, but in a bustling hospital like this, no one was likely to acknowledge that we'd walked through the doors.

I started to the left and the elevator bank that waited for us there. Peter kept up and the three of us —four if you counted Dinah—stepped in. A young doctor slid in as the doors closed.

"Oh man, almost got the pinch there!" He pushed up a set of glasses on his nose and straightened his overcoat. He had short dark hair and a smooth face that made me think he was barely out of his teens.

Young, so young and fresh and he had no idea who and what he stood next to in the elevator. His nametag read Dr. Lee.

"I'm a new nurse," I said. "What floor is the X-ray machine on?"

"Oh, that's the subbasement. You're going down for that." He hit the appropriate button and flashed a smile at me. I made myself smile back.

"Thank you."

"No problem."

I waited for him to ask what we needed the X-ray for, but he didn't. I'd take a bit of luck thrown our way.

He got off on the third floor and then we were headed back down. The doors opened on our floor and we stepped out.

"I don't really need the help now," Cowboy said.

"It's part of the image," I said. "I'm a nurse, you're a patient."

"Sexy nurse helps wounded cowboy," Dinah mused. "Not as kinky as I like it, but sure, we could run with that show."

I rolled my eyes, but secretly had to fight a laugh. "I missed you too, Dinah."

"Bitch, you didn't have wax stuck in you for the last year," she said. "I've gotta make up for lost time."

"I had someone monitoring my every thought," I said. "I win the shit year award."

"Fine," she muttered. "You win this time."

Peter stayed close behind me, guarding our rear. I didn't look back at him. I didn't have to.

We were in this together, the three of us, for good or for bad, till death did we part.

That thought did make me smile, which was good since we'd reached the nurse's desk. She looked up as we drew close, and her smile answered mine.

"Which doctor sent you down?"

"Dr. Lee," I said.

She frowned as she looked over her paper. "I don't see it here. Maybe he hasn't had a chance to send the order down."

We didn't have time to sweet-talk her, nor did I have the inclination, so I moved around the desk and pulled Dinah out, pressing her against the nurse's back. "Move real quiet. You're going to help us run the machine now."

Her back stiffened and I helped her stand. She had boxed blond hair that wasn't fooling anyone with the dark roots, and her body was less than firm. Early fifties was my guess. I didn't hold those things against her, but they assured me she was no threat. No FBI agent in hiding. No monster in the closet.

"I can't do X-rays," she said. "We need a tech."

I motioned at her to pick up the phone. "So call a tech."

Peter took a step back and then another. "The elevator. I can jam it."

"Wait till the tech gets here," I said.

The nurse picked up the phone, her hand trembling so hard she could barely lift it. I watched her dial through and pressed the button to put the call on speaker phone. She swallowed hard.

"Easy," I leaned over to see her name, "Lacey. Easy. We won't hurt anyone, but we need the X-rays. Nice and simple."

She nodded jerkily, and the phone clicked through. She stuttered through her request for an X-ray tech to come down to the subbasement, but the guy on the other end didn't seem bothered. A few minutes later, he strode out of the elevator.

Older than I thought he'd be, the tech had the appearance of a grumpy old man who probably yelled at people to get off his lawn on weekends, and seemed irritated he'd been called to run a machine no one else could run. "Lacey, what kind of emergency is this anyway?"

Pete stepped in behind him and the sound of tearing metal ripped through the air. The tech turned and looked at Pete as the Magelore held out a handful of wires. "Consider it permanently parked."

"Block the stairs," I said as I turned toward the

tech, touching his chest with the tip of Dinah's muzzle. "Name?"

He looked down at the gun and then back up at me, his eyes narrowing. "Carlos."

"Well, Carlos, today is your lucky day. You get to run three full body X-rays faster than you ever have before. Just for shits and giggles."

I moved him with a flick of Dinah, and for his age, he stepped fast. Perhaps it was the gun.

Worry that someone was listening to my thoughts, my words, itched at the back of my neck like an errant bug intent on burrowing under my skin, but I shook it off. "Cowboy, you first. Pete, watch the nurse at the front."

Peter gave me a nod and stayed out of the room.

"He needs to be naked," Carlos said as he set up the machine. "It'll go faster that way."

I stood between the two men as Cowboy stripped down to his boxers.

"Leave those," Carlos said, not an ounce of fear in him. Interesting. Very interesting.

I stood behind the screen, watching as X-ray after X-ray was taken. Five in all. Carlos was efficient, I'd give him that.

"You aren't afraid of us," I said as he started to pull the images up on his computer.

Carlos glanced at me. "You are abnormals, yes?"

I nodded. "Yes."

He blinked a few times, then wiped his face. "My daughter went missing six months ago. She moved like you, like a predator always on the hunt. Except the people she hunted were those who preyed on the weak, and she worked with the police. She would not just leave the way the police say she did."

The images flickered to life and he tapped the screen. "What are you looking for?"

"A small tracking device. More than one, likely," I said.

Carlos found the first one. "There. In the back of his left knee. A strange place."

"Hard to get out," I said. "It's inside the joint."

The other one was not so easy to pinpoint. "There, is that one in the soft tissue behind his right ear?" I touched the screen and the image magnified with one touch.

"Yes, that one could be removed easily." Carlos nodded. "You all have them?"

"No idea," I said.

I stripped off my clothes as Cowboy stepped into the room with Carlos. I handed Dinah to Cowboy. "Don't shoot Carlos. He's got a daughter like us."

Cowboy grunted and I made my way out to the padded table and lay down. Carlos moved around me, setting up the X-ray and the machine whirred to life. Click, click, click.

"Pictures are done," Carlos called out.

I sat up and went to the smaller room, scooped Dinah from Cowboy, and made my way back to the receptionist desk as I pulled my clothing back on. Peter sat at the desk, the nurse sprawled in his arms, blood running down her neck.

"Really? I said watch her, not eat her."

He grunted and rolled his eyes to me, eyes that widened as they took in my semi-bare-ass state. "You or her. Haven't eaten in a long time. Not properly. I'll be honest, you taste like honey."

"You hear that noise?"

"Hmm. Someone is banging on the door." He bent his head over her neck and she let out a long moan.

"Dude, this is not the time!" Dinah snapped.

"Don't kill her," I said as I strode by the desk toward the stairwell. The frosted glass in the door showed movement beyond it.

"X-ray machine, now!" I growled at Peter. "Or I leave you behind."

"Fuck," he growled, but he set the nurse on the floor and ran to the back room. I moved around the desk and did a quick search. The light blinked rapidly on the phone and I scooped up the receiver.

"Hello?"

"Lacey, what the hell is going on down there?"

"Well, we seem to have a stuck door and a stuck elevator. But we're all good. No patients down here,

just me and Carlos." *Lacey and Carlos, sitting in a tree .
. .*

"Jesus, we couldn't get through, we thought . . .
there was a breakout at Clearview Rehabilitation
Center, and they said three of the inmates were
headed this general direction. It's all over the emergency alert channels on everyone's phones even so
it's a doozy."

I sat in the chair, kept my voice smooth. "Oh,
well, we're good. Just fix the elevator. I don't fancy
doing stairs for the rest of my shift. I'm not as young
as I used to be, you know."

The guy on the other end of the phone barked a
laugh and hung up, but not before I heard him say,
"They're all good. Just the usual shit with the maintenance on this place."

I'd noticed a TV behind the nurse's desk earlier,
and a quick search produced a remote. When I
flicked on the TV, Cowboy showed up next to me.
"Find a news channel," I said.

He went through a few stations before he landed
on something worthy of the word "news." An aerial
shot of a chunk of forest panned over until it picked
up a massive gray stone building, the same color as
the walls I'd stared at for the last year.

"Turn it up."

A woman broadcaster's voice filled the room.

"According to officials, three inmates broke out of

the maximum-security facility earlier tonight. Two deaths are being reported, one guard and one of the counselors."

Two pictures popped up on the screen, one of George smiling, holding up a drink with a hand he no longer had, and one of what must have been Eligor, though he was tagged as Dr. Ernest Snathy and looked completely different. Just a tallish man with a receding hairline and glasses.

"They are driving a dark blue truck, stolen from the Clearview Rehabilitation Center, and are considered extremely dangerous. If you see this truck," a perfect image of the truck we'd been driving flashed on the screen, "do not approach them. Call 9-1-1 immediately and stay as far away from them as possible."

"Fuck," Cowboy said. "We need to change vehicles."

"We would have anyway," I said.

Carlos and Peter came back into the room. Carlos stared hard at Lacey. "Is she alive?"

"Yes, but she'll have a real hangover tomorrow," Peter said.

Carlos flipped printouts of the X-rays onto the desk. "You two gringos, your cases are simple. Two tracers in you that I can see." He tapped the knee and neck on the X-rays of what I assumed were the two men. "You, though," he gave me a look and pulled my X-rays out, spreading them across the desk. "I have never seen so many."

"Holy shit." Peter leaned over the image. "Just in this one shot I can see twenty, maybe twenty-five."

Carlos nodded. "All her images are like this. You have one large one behind your ear like the other two, but that is a decoy, I think." Smart man. I agreed with him.

We had to fry the tracers, and we had to do it fast. There would be no getting the ones out of our knees. No way to get all of them out of me, assuming we even managed to start.

"Let me think." I stepped away from the desk, tapping Dinah against my leg as I walked down the hall away from the three men. "Dinah."

"Yeah?"

"Any ideas?"

She was quiet a moment. "If Killian were here, I'd say have him run you through with a bolt of electricity. But he's not, and the breakers . . ."

"They'll switch off before we get hit with enough juice to do the job. The EMP that Cowboy can produce is a possibility." I turned to look at Cowboy. "Think you can pulse enough juice through us to fry the tracers?"

He swallowed. "I can try. But I'm . . . it's like I'm blocked." He closed his eyes and after a tense minute that felt a hell of a lot longer where nothing happened, he shook his head. "I got nothing."

Damn.

I turned and paced toward the reception desk, past the dark rooms of what was essentially the guts of the hospital. The X-ray machine likely didn't bother the tracers.

A sign caught my eye and I stopped in front of it. *Remove all metal piercings and jewelry. Alert technician to any metal pins you have.*

I pointed at the sign. "Magnetic Radio Imaging. Would that work?"

Carlos hurried toward me. "This is a new machine, very powerful. We have not tested it on any RFIDs."

Cowboy looked at him. "What?"

"Radio frequency identification," I said, then looked at Carlos. "You test on them?"

He shrugged. "To make sure that the people tagged with them are safe when they go through. But that was the old machines. This one is higher tech and can give details the others couldn't."

"Magnetic interference could disrupt the guts of the tracers though, couldn't it?" I was nodding even as I asked the question.

Carlos puckered his face. "Yes, I believe this machine would do that. We have to keep all cell phones far from it. The few that have gone in the room by accident had their computers completely fried."

"Are you sure?" Cowboy pushed up beside me.

It was a childish question, and I refused to answer it. But I also refused to consider the possibility this wouldn't work. If it didn't . . . well, if it didn't, Dinah was going to have only a few last shots in her.

"Who is first?" Peter said. "I can handle pain, but if it's not going to work, I'm not doing it."

"Me first," I said. "You two next. Dinah, hang with Cowboy a bit," I said, handing her over.

"Only if he tucks me in his waistband. I'm betting on a tattoo on his ass," she snickered. I pushed the door open and they followed me in.

One way or another, we were stopping those bastards from the facility from following us.

9

ELIGOR FLOATED IN A STATE OF SEMI-CONSCIOUSNESS. He'd been dragged out of the little body that had been his vessel for the last ten years as they'd prepped to deal with the abnormals. Not that he was surprised it had been taken from him. That was what he got for turning on his own kind.

What a fool he'd been to think one of those monsters was not a monster. She'd fooled him, and . . . that was that. He'd believed she was kind and thoughtful, and he'd believed her lies. Maybe he should've been more like Susan. Maybe he should've been harder on them.

If he'd had a body, he would have groaned at that thought. He didn't *want* to be like Susan. No. That was not his way. He would never let it be his way. Better to be a trusting fool than to be cruel. No doubt, he'd be bottled up in Gardreel's storage room for the rest of eternity, stuck.

So certain was he that he'd be terminated, it came as a bit of a shock when a sound slipped out of him. He blinked and slowly lifted his head, opened his eyes, and stared at what was in front of him.

Glasses slid down his nose and he lifted a hand to push them back up. "What . . . is happening?"

The person who stood in front of him was as much of a shock as the noise he'd made. Her red hair was twisted off to one side, showing off a freshly shaved portion of her head. Green eyes locked on him as she lifted what at first he thought was a stick, and pointed it at him. No, not a stick.

"That wand was broken when you were brought in," he whispered.

"Ah, yes, so it was." She ran a hand over it, up and down in a way that he didn't understand but knew was supposed to be provocative. "But I fixed it."

His eyes widened and he searched the room. "What is happening?"

"Oh, well, I've been given a job," she said. "And you're going to help me."

Eligor swallowed hard and pushed to his feet. Not four feet tall anymore. The world gave a nause-ating lurch as he stumbled around on legs that were practically as long as he'd been tall previously.

"Jesus Christ, what's wrong with you?" Easter snapped.

"Not Jesus Christ, about as far from that as possible. My name is Eligor." He put a hand on the back of the chair he'd been reclined in. "How am I here? How am I not . . . finished?"

She quirked a bright red eyebrow up. "You have a connection to Phoenix, don't you?"

"Well, yes and no—"

"Even without the token?"

"Yes, but—"

"And that means you can find her."

"Not the way—"

She reached out and jabbed the point of her wand against his heart. "You can find her, or we're both going back into that hell hole. Your mind stripped out of this body and cast into nothing, and my mind shattered by whatever torture they want to use on me."

She adjusted herself, a flicker in her eyes that Eligor knew. Susan hadn't let this one go, and even without the touchstone object, her mind was so broken she could be easily controlled. No, Susan hadn't let her go, not in the least.

But Easter thought she was free.

His heart pounded. "So why do they need us? Those that escaped are loaded with tracers in their bodies. A guarantee of finding them." That was how it was supposed to work. Then the Brutes would go after them.

He shuddered at the thought.

Easter looked him over. "Phoenix is smart. She fooled you for a year, didn't she? You think tracers will slow her?"

Eligor didn't so much as blink. Admitting he'd been fooled was such a dumb idea—even a dupe like him knew not to agree with it.

She smiled, a sharp, predatory smile that reached her eyes and made them gleam with a light that was rather unsettling. "Why do you think they unleashed me? Because of my good behavior? They kept my hatred of her alive for this very possibility."

He shook his head. "I have no idea—"

"Because she has already managed to find a way to cut off all the tracers they put in her. Sixty-six of them, and they all deactivated at once."

Eligor gaped. If he'd known that was possible, he would have gone with her. The reality was, he hadn't thought they'd make it more than a few miles before being scooped up, and he had thought only to buy her a little more time.

"What about the other two with her?"

"Them too. All tracers gone. That is a very bad thing for this place, isn't it? To have abnormals out there that know and understand, at least to some degree, what is happening here." She looked like she was about to say something else, but her eyes blanked out and he knew he was talking to Susan.

Her smile was manufactured. "Eligor, you will go with this abnormal. You will help her find the Phoenix and her friends. You will kill the two men. And you will bring the Phoenix back here."

He stared at Easter. "Wait, you don't want her dead?"

"No." Her voice was flat, monotone. "You will bring her back here. Easter will help you as she is the only one with skills that even come close to the Phoenix's abilities."

He found it interesting that the names the two abnormals had come in with were being used, not the names the handlers had given them, slip-ups just like he'd had. With difficulty, he kept his mouth shut and his throat from bobbing.

She stared at him. "You understand that your life will be in extreme danger while you hunt the Phoenix."

"I am not a fighter. That's what the Brutes are for," he said.

"You will have this." Easter held up a wristband and handed it to him. He took it and dangled it from one finger. She went on. "There is an emergency setting that will bring the Brutes to your aid when you manage to trap the Phoenix."

Eligor put the wristband on and it tightened automatically around his rather thick wrist. "You speak about her as if she is—"

Easter waved a hand at him and her eyes came back to life as Susan checked out. "Nix—Phoenix to you—is the most dangerous abnormal alive. She has been trained to kill since she was a child, and her kill count is in the thousands. She has killed demons, Magelores, and other abnormals no one else would dare even face. She has encyclopedic knowledge of weapons, explosives, guerrilla warfare tactics, body armor, and torture tactics as well as a strong connection to the mob world and the world of abnormal magic."

His jaw flapped open. "I know that was on her papers when she came in, but I saw none of that in her head! None of it!"

"Exactly." Easter slid her wand through a belt loop on her right side. "She is good enough that she fooled a mind reader. Or whatever the fuck you are."

He didn't realize he was shaking until the thumping of the chair legs on the floor made him look down. His grip on the back of the chair was white-knuckled and he couldn't stop himself. "She was truly all those things?"

Easter laughed, her eyes lighting up. "She *is* all those things and more, Eligor. You want to know a secret?"

He wasn't sure he wanted to know any more

secrets. He couldn't wrap his head around the fact that the woman he'd been helping this last year was . . . evil. Because if what Easter had said was true, there was no other word for it. Except he couldn't shake his certain feeling that she'd genuinely wanted to help the other abnormals in the facility. He'd seen her soul, and it was dark, brilliantly dark, but not evil.

He couldn't be fooled, not like that. Maybe she'd kept secrets from him, but her intentions had an undeniable purity to them. Slowly the shaking stopped. "Yes, tell me the secret."

Easter smirked. "You're going to be traveling with someone... Just. Like. Her."

———

Carlisle Hospital faded in the rearview mirror as Carlos drove us slowly away, staying well within the speed limit. Behind us, the hospital was lit up like a Christmas tree, and a series of large trucks peeled toward the parking lot only minutes after we left.

"My Rosita, was she in that facility?" He glanced at me, then back to the dark road in front of us, ignoring what was behind.

I shivered, not because I was afraid, but because there was nowhere on my body that didn't sing as if I'd been stuck inside a medieval torture chamber and had hot spikes driven into me. The boys rubbed at their necks and knees, but my entire body hummed with heat and pain.

"No, she wasn't there. I met all those who came in after me. There was no Rosita; they always changed our names to something similar, and no one came in that was Hispanic with an R name," I said.

His second question was no surprise. "Could you find her? I could get you a picture and I could pay. I have money."

I breathed through another ripple of muscle tremors before I answered.

"Possibly. Cowboy thinks there are other facilities like this one," I said. "But I have to find my own boy, Carlos. He's young, not even fourteen years old."

"I'll send you with a picture," he said, the pain in his voice audible. "And if you find her . . . please. Just get her out. Please? I helped you."

He choked up on that last word and I closed my eyes, hating his pain. A father's pain, a mother's love, I understood that. I clenched my jaw, fighting off the part of me that wanted to ease his hurt. Caring about other people's pain was a good way to lose everyone I loved.

My boy had been taken from me once, and I had thought he was dead. For a long time, I'd lived in a fog, believing he'd been killed in a hit meant for me. But I'd found him. I'd found him, and I'd found

Killian, a man I'd thought would stand beside me through anything that came our way. He had stood beside me until that last night.

The night he'd let me go.

My eyes snapped open, and I stared at the road in front of us, refusing to relive that memory. The shakes continued and I wondered if it was all from the machine or the distant memories trying to surface. I rubbed at my arms, trying to banish a phantom itch.

"Withdrawal from the drugs they had you on," Peter said. "You've got all the symptoms. Irritability, itching, paranoia." He grinned. "Maybe you were always like that?"

Dinah piped up. "Irritable and paranoid, yes, but that comes with the territory."

"They take us when we're sleeping, so we have to sleep in shifts." I changed the subject. Not because I thought the Magelore was wrong, but because there was nothing I could do but ride it out.

Cowboy and Peter nodded. Carlos looked at me again. I was in the front passenger seat, my dog's head in my lap, Dinah clutched in my left hand.

"Left-handed?" Carlos asked.

"Both," Dinah replied for me. "She's faster with her left, though."

Cowboy leaned forward. "Didn't you have two

guns? I thought it was always two in the stories I heard."

I missed having two guns. Missed having Eleanor there to be the hard line when I needed her. "Yeah, I did. One was destroyed."

Destroyed saving me.

"You should get another," Carlos said quietly. It struck me that he was totally unfazed by the fact that my gun had just spoken. He hadn't reacted earlier, either, to her comment about Cowboy. I twisted in my seat with a grimace as a cold shiver ran through me, followed by a serious hot flash.

"Carlos." I stared at the side of his face, at the complete lack of nerves he was showing. Something had felt off about him from the very beginning. Too cool around abnormals and the way he'd given us the story about his daughter had rung true but also . . . not. I drew a deep breath, but he didn't smell like an abnormal.

"Yes?"

I stared at him, my thoughts whipping around faster and faster. "Who are you really?"

"I am Carlos." He didn't take his eyes off the road, but he frowned. "I'm not sure who else I could be?"

Peter snort-laughed. "Phoenix, you're too paranoid. He's human. I can smell it all over him."

Except the most powerful abnormals didn't smell

feral or wild like the weaker ones. In fact, they smelled just like a human. Like nothing.

I had Dinah up and pressed against Carlos's head before another heartbeat passed. "Pull over."

He did as I said, cool as a summer breeze. "It is not as you think, Nix."

Nix.

The name only my friends dared to call me.

Carlos turned the car off, and as the engine idled to nothing, I lowered Dinah.

"Who and *what* are you?"

"Rio would like to speak with you," he said, and his image wavered, the aura around him sparkling and dancing like a heatwave over a road. A Hider was an abnormal who could mask his own abilities to appear human, and a strong Hider could also mask those around him. I'd seen the ability before. My surrogate father, Zee, had been a Hider, and one of the very best. He'd given me almost eleven years living as a mother to Bear before I'd lost him.

Cowboy gave a low whistle. "A Hider! Shit, dude, you . . ."

"That's why they didn't find us at the hospital," I said, the pieces of that tiny puzzle slipping into place. "You'd be about the only kind of abnormal safe from a purge like what has been happening here in North America."

He nodded. "But it wasn't enough to keep my

daughter safe. She was too determined to help others, to try to figure out why this was happening and stop it. Her partner in the local department, he has been hunting for her with no luck. I sent him to New York. That seems to be where the last of the abnormals are in hiding."

I frowned. "Can you hide all three of us?"

"For tonight, then you must get to Rio. He is in New York too."

I went over what I knew about Rio in my head. At the time I'd stepped away from my father's business, Rio had been a small fry, barely a blip on the radar. Prostitution was his main money maker, hidden behind three strip clubs, but he'd dabbled in some money laundering. That was the minor connection he'd had to my father, washing the money as it came through the clubs.

That had been a long time ago, though—when I'd stormed back into the picture looking for vengeance, there hadn't been even a whisper of the Latin mob boss. Again though, I hadn't been looking for Rio then. I'd been looking for Mancini and my father.

Peter shook his head. "No, I'm not going to New York. They'll be looking for us there. It's a fucking hotbed of abnormals. Or it was."

Carlos motioned at the car. "May we continue? My wife has dinner waiting for us. Late, but I think you three need a good meal."

"Already eaten, thanks," Peter said with a pointed grin.

I eased back in my seat. "Drive."

Dinah settled on my lap and the dog got comfortable too. I traced her scars—the bite marks, but also several cuts from a razor-sharp knife. Those scars were perfect, clean, and as numerous as the ones from other dogs.

It felt weird, like touching my own skin, tracing my scars.

She sighed and melted into my lap.

Much as I wanted Carlos to talk to me, I didn't actually trust Peter or Cowboy. I was no fool. They were not my friends. Current partners, yes, but not friends.

In the real world, the Magelore and I would have tried to kill each other ten times over by now. And Cowboy? I would have walked by the squeaky-clean kid without a second look. He wasn't part of our world of darkness and death. Or at least he shouldn't be, despite his abilities. At the same time, I knew my odds at finding my boy would be better if they tagged along. Their odds of survival would be better too. If I left the kid behind, he'd be bagged and tagged again in no time. Peter might last longer, but not by much. He'd been taken near the beginning of the purge, not long after me as far as I could see.

Carlos drove through a lovely suburban area lit

up with fake tiki torches and summer patio lanterns on most houses.

"Nice," Peter said. "You really live here?"

"Benefits of being a Hider," Carlos said.

My thoughts moved rapidly as we slid out of the car and followed him into his house. His wife was a petite woman whose curves met in the middle with a waist strapped in with a big buckled belt over her flowered dress. A perfect little housewife down to the styled hair and manicured nails. Very human looking. She smiled up at us, but I saw the strain in her eyes.

And the power that glittered back at me telling me she was stronger even than her husband.

"Two Hiders," I said.

She gave a slow nod. "Come in. Eat and talk. You are safe here."

Eat and talk, if only this was going to be that easy.

10

"Tell me exactly what happened from the beginning. I was taken before I heard anything about a purge," I said as we sat at the oversized dinner table in Carlos and Anita's house.

She had laid out a full meal with soup, salad, a main course of roast beef and potatoes, and a selection of other dishes I just glanced at. Much as my stomach growled and my body shook with the withdrawal from the drugs, I needed information as much as I needed a plate of real food. Cowboy knew some stuff, but he didn't strike me as understanding the ebb and flow of the abnormal world. This couple had ties to the mob and the police. They'd have more information.

I slid a stack of beef and potatoes onto a plate and lowered it to the floor for the dog. I really needed to name her.

Carlos folded his hands on the table and spoke quietly. "It started before the public knew there was going to be a purge of abnormals. As you know, the strongest abnormals were taken as quickly and as quietly as they could be taken, mostly in their sleep using an airborne mist that suppressed not only their minds, but their abilities.

"The heads of the mob families were targeted, and Rio barely escaped. Mostly with our help, but that is not to brag. It is to say that with two Hiders of our strength helping him, he was nearly caught."

Chills rippled through me and my skin rose in goose flesh. No one was eating apart from the dog and Cowboy.

"When the bill was passed, it was unanimous. Abnormals had been acknowledged in the past but were not openly accepted. We had our place in certain parts of every town. We were outsiders, but there was no real issue. A certain flavor of hatred and fear that most normals barely held contained."

The boys nodded. I didn't move.

"The bill stated that abnormals were hiding in plain sight and were manipulating the government. Senators Rylee, Alexander, and Ashspur were all immediately outed as abnormals and taken."

Well, shit. That explained that side of things.

"Taken where? They weren't in our facility," I said.

Carlos shook his head. "I don't know. Rosita was looking for them when she went missing. When they took her."

He handed me a picture of his daughter. Dark-haired with deeply intense amber eyes, she was younger than me by a few years and would stand out in any crowd with her natural beauty and the curves she'd inherited from her mother. She hadn't been in our facility, but I already knew that. I held the picture. "Go on."

Carlos spread his hands on the table. "After that, abnormals were scooped up left and right. The majority of humans didn't even seem to understand what was happening or why. The bill was vague at best, but it gave the government the right to remove abnormals from society."

"With no reason?"

He nodded. "Zero reason. Specially trained and equipped squads were sent out at night, and they used the airborne mist to knock out entire apartment buildings so they could scoop up the abnormals. I saw it happen once, so it is not a rumor."

His story rang of truth, but there was something missing. "Someone has to be heading this up. Who is it? Which senator?"

"As far as we can tell, no one. The bill was put

forward and was passed, but when we tried to find out who had done it, there was no senator behind it. It just showed up and they passed it. The facility you were in was the only one I knew about at the time. Which is why I got the job at the hospital. I hoped they would bring an injured abnormal in for treatment. Rio agreed it was a good plan. I never expected to find three escapees. And certainly not you, Nix."

His wife put her hand to her mouth. "The Phoenix?"

I nodded.

Dinah laughed. "She had her wings clipped. Shocking, isn't it?"

"Shut it, Dinah." I slapped a hand over her.

Anita put her hand to her chest. "I knew Zee. He trained me."

That stuck a sharp stab right through my heart. "He died protecting me," I said softly. "He used too much ability and lost his mind." That was the nice way of putting it, but I wasn't going to give her the details of his death. Not here, not now.

She closed her eyes and a tear slid from one. Either she was an extraordinary actress, or she was truly hurt by that news.

Call me cruel, but part of me wondered if it was an act. I'd been duped by tears a few times, so I didn't like to give too much weight to them and the emotions they evoked.

"And now?"

"The squads still make regular hits on different buildings, but they're taking in fewer prisoners each time. The abnormals left on the streets are savvy and avoiding them easier and easier. But they are still being taken," Carlos said. "How many new abnormals do you get?"

"They just fill in the blanks when one dies." I tapped one finger on the table. "There was no one new in our neck of the woods other than Cowboy here." I tipped my head toward the kid.

"You sure he's not a plant?" Anita asked.

I snorted. "Because they knew we were going to break out? That I'd have a soft spot for the kid? No, they were in our heads but not in mine like that."

Now it was my turn to fill them in, and I did as quickly as I could. The fingers in our minds, the blank looks, the guards, and Eligor.

"I know that name," Anita said. She turned and grabbed a book, the name scrawled out on it popping out to me. Demonology.

I nodded. "Me too. I believe . . . it's the name of a demon. I'm sure of it—I studied them after my last run-in. Demons doing this makes sense, but they still must have someone driving them. The other names he mentioned I'm not as sure of. But Eligor, I am." I could already see the players lining up. "If I were to guess right now and lay money on it, I would say that someone has called in a big player, a powerful demon who has his own underlings, and the demon is eliminating anyone who could stand in his way. Once the abnormals are locked up, who can stop the demons? A human priest? Doubtful. All the good priests were abnormals hiding in plain sight."

"This is why you need to go see Rio. He has connections to the few others still in play. A Hider is helping him. She's young but strong."

My only plan was to go to New York to find intel on Killian. I was going after my son, not some demon on a vendetta.

A wash of fatigue hit me hard and I closed my eyes, breathing through it. Anita noticed first. "They are exhausted, Carlos. Come, I will show you where you can sleep. Carlos and I will hide this place for the night so you can all sleep in peace. But you must go in the morning."

Peter followed her as if he were a well-trained pup. A Magelore sleeping peacefully in the same house as me, under the protection of a couple of Hiders. I wouldn't have guessed I'd be ending my day this way if I'd had a million guesses.

Cowboy stretched and then leaned across the table to me. "You trust the Magelore?" he asked in an undertone.

"About as much as I trust you," I said.

Dinah laughed and Cowboy drew back as if I'd slapped him. "Seriously?"

"I didn't say I didn't trust either of you. I said I trust you the same." I reached for the food on the table and filled my plate. I needed food, real food, and then I would sleep.

Anita led a sullen Cowboy to another room so it was just me and Carlos at the table. I shoved food in my mouth, moaning as the flavors hit my tongue.

"Good stuff." Carlos smiled as he cupped a coffee mug in his hands. "My Anita is quite a cook." I kept on shoveling as he watched, his eyes sad. "If you are right about the demons, we are in deep trouble. But you will look for Rosita? When you are stopping this? Keep an eye out for her at least?"

I slowed my chewing and spoke around a mouthful of food. Telling him I wasn't going after Rosita was a bad idea, so I figured I'd sidestep the question. "I need to check a few things, but I can find out if it's a demon real quick." I paused, then asked, "Are the tracers really destroyed?" The MRI machine had been almost too slick, too easy. And they found us at the hospital.

His smile slid off his face. "Yes. They are out of commission. But I hid you from the moment I realized who you were, what you were. It bought us time. Likely the vehicle you were driving had a tracer too. That is where I'd lay my guess."

"Why did you hide what you were from us?" I asked.

"I was trying to protect my wife. You are known for your shoot first and never bother to ask questions style of working. I hoped that we would be able to appeal to you to go after our daughter. I have heard the stories of how you took down Mancini to save your own son."

I tapped a finger on the table again. "That was when I worked for my father, I had no pull then. It was not my job to ask questions."

"So you are a freelance assassin now?" His eyebrows shot up.

I sighed and kept eating. "I am a mother whose children are missing, Carlos. The same as yours."

Children. No. Child. My gut clenched and I snapped my teeth shut to keep the food in my belly.

Carlos reached across the table and put a hand on top of mine. "My Rosita, I saw her the day before she went missing. You see from the picture she has her mother's beauty and fire? She was determined to help the missing abnormals. Many of them were her friends. Those she'd grown up with. Good people."

I stared at him as he stared down at the picture of his daughter. Her long dark hair had been caught up in the wind, and really, she looked like a model as she smiled coyly over her shoulder at the camera. Unusually bright amber eyes peered out from under long dark lashes, sparkling with laughter, with life.

"She said she had a lead. It didn't take her to the facility that you were at, but somewhere else. She went there and now . . . she is gone. Her partner couldn't find a trace of her. He has all her papers. Maybe together you two could—"

I was already shaking my head. "That's not how this works."

He barreled on as if I hadn't spoken. "I wanted you to feel a connection to her so you would want to find her for us," he whispered. "You are the Phoenix. You are the boogeyman of our world. If you cannot save us, who will?"

His fingers tightened on mine and I turned my hand over so we were palm to palm. "Please, find her."

"Fuck," I said. "I can't help anyone. Don't you get it? If they can do this to all our kind, what hope do I have of stopping them? None. That is the answer. None. They locked me up as if it were nothing, Carlos. Me."

I'd seen Bear in trouble. My boy was afraid and angry, and that was what had driven me out of the facility more than anything else. My tolerance for waiting, for biding my time, had exploded in an instant. Nothing mattered more than my boy's safety.

Because he was the only one I had left.

"I was giving birth," I found myself telling him. "When they took me."

Anita walked into the room and sat, a small box in her lap.

Dinah was quiet, and I could feel her listening. She hadn't known I was pregnant with Killian's child when I gave her to Easter.

"They did not use the mist?" Carlos asked.

"I was awake. They gave me an epidural for a C-section. Tied my arms down. Strapped my head back. I let them, of course, I did." I started to shake, unable to stop the memories now as I slowly spoke through them.

My head was strapped to the operating room table as were my arms. Lower body numbed and useless from the epidural. But I could hear, and that torture was like nothing I'd ever felt before.

I could hear and do nothing as my world turned itself inside out.

"Tell him," one of the nurses said. "We've got no pulse on the child. None on the mother."

There was no cry of a baby, no first breath taken. Hands pushed on my innards as I was roughly put back together. I wanted to speak, to tell them they were wrong. I was alive. I was sure the baby was too. She was alive. She had to be.

I tried to pull on my wrists, needing to get up, but my body ignored me. The cold flush from the epidural spread through me again, up and down my spine, paralyzing me. A cold cloth settled over my eyes, cutting out the bright lights of the surgical room. I couldn't even twist my head side to side. A set of hands pushed down on either wrist, holding me there. "You don't want to move. They're still stitching you up."

The cloth didn't come off my eyes. Killian's voice echoed to me. "I need to see her."

My heart lurched. He would get me out of this nightmare. Our girl could not have died, and I knew I was not dead. I heard the cry of an infant from far away and tried to jerk on the ties holding me down. The cloth on my eyes slid off and I was looking up into his face, into his green eyes. The words wouldn't come, though. I had no voice as I fought whatever was sliding through me, whatever drug they were pumping into my spine to keep me immobile.

Killian. Don't let them take me.

Because that was what was going to happen. Someone was taking me. I didn't know why, but I knew this game as surely as I knew my own name. As surely as I knew anything in my life.

"Nix," Killian whispered my name, touched my face, then closed his eyes. "Go then. Take her."

Take her.

Was he out of his mind? A scream bubbled up in me, but nothing came out, as if I had no control over my body at all. There were fingers in my mind keeping me still, keeping me quiet. Killian turned away, a child in his arms.

Maybe she'd survived? But his next words negated that.
"I'll bury them together."

Together.

I only had to say one word, to tell them to stop, and I knew I could change his mind. Why would he tell them to take me?

"Finally. That man was far too good for an abnormal whore like this one."

A woman had said that. A nurse maybe? I didn't know, didn't care. I tried again to pull against the straps, over and over, but my body didn't react to my commands and I didn't know how to get around the drugs in my system.

"She's trying to burn through it."

"The handlers will have her soon enough. Give her a heavy dose, it won't kill her."

Something was shot into my IV. The tingle started in my left arm and spread upward to my chest and then into my lungs, slowing my breathing. But I was still awake, even if I couldn't move a fucking inch.

Where were they taking me, and why?

Away from my family, that was where. Rage lit me up and the drugs dissipated as if they'd never been in me. I snapped the straps holding me down.

"Damn it, hold her!"

"I can't. She's too strong!"

The shouts were music to my ears as I fought the five men who had thought they could manhandle me into a waiting vehicle. My legs were still unresponsive, but my upper body was doing just fine, even with a brand-new C-section incision stitched up tight. I didn't feel it, not through the rage that kept me moving.

I punched the one on my left in an uppercut to the balls. He went down and I pulled his weapon—a Taser. I shot it into the guy to my right and he jerked and bounced like a fish on the line.

The problem was there were too many of them, and not enough of me. Someone grabbed me from behind and put me into a sleeper choke. If my legs had been functioning, I could have . . . the thought stuttered as the blood cut off to my head. But that wasn't what really slowed me.

No, the fingers in my mind were what cut me off from anything I could do.

I slapped at the hands and went limp. I was released and stuffed into an ambulance, or some other similar transport, strapped down to a board, and my IV was jammed into a new bag of something. I stared up at it, blood trickling down the side of my face. An attendant got in with me, lifted my shirt.

"Shit, she ripped the stitches."

One of those holding me stepped up and sat next to me. My head was again strapped to the board so all I could do was roll my eyes to look at him. He looked to be in his forties, strong build, square bulky jaw like a bulldog. Marine if I was reading him right. At the very least, he was a marine.

He stared down at me. "You aren't ever going to get

out of where you are going. So you'd best stop trying." His nametag said George.

I didn't answer him. That was what he wanted.

He settled beside me while the paramedic, or whoever it was, stitched me up. Nurse maybe? My brain tried to tell me that a paramedic wouldn't be stitching me up.

The marine smiled. "You got that look like a caged animal. I'm going to recommend some things to make your stay easier on all of us."

"I'll kill you," I whispered.

"You might think that." He didn't stop smiling, but instead pulled a pack of cigarettes from a pocket and put one in his mouth.

The paramedic/nurse shook his head but didn't tell the marine not to smoke in that small area where I had no doubt an oxygen tank was hidden somewhere. Maybe he'd blow us all up.

"You see, the handlers want you bad." The marine drew in a drag, held it, and puffed out a perfect ring. "They think you're special, but I think you're just like all the other freakshows."

"You aren't supposed to talk to her," the nurse said.

"The meds they've got will wipe her memory of this." The marine blew smoke into my face. "And this bitch killed two of my men. So let me have my fun."

He leaned over and pulled his cigarette from his mouth, close enough that he could have kissed me. He lifted the cigarette to my eye. "You don't need to see to do what they need you to do."

I twisted my head hard to one side and the strap on my forehead slid off. I snapped my head forward, catching him on the bridge of the nose, shattering it. He fell back with a yell, pulled a gun and leveled it at me.

"Don't you do it," the nurse said. "We'll both get eliminated if we lose her."

The marine was breathing hard, blood flowing from his nose as I stared up at him. "I'll kill you."

What felt like days later, we stopped, and I was pulled out of the transport vehicle. The light was bright on my eyes and I blinked away tears as I looked up at the building we approached. Or rather I was pushed toward, still strapped down.

The sign on the front glass door had a different name then, one that they changed later.

Clearview Medical Institute for the Criminally Insane.

11

"Dios mio." Anita was the first to speak after my voice faded. "So you had a daughter? She lived?"

"No." I fought to keep my voice free of emotional inflections after speaking about what was no doubt the worst memory of my life, and that was saying something.

"We knew Killian had taken up with you," Carlos said. "We did our best to keep tabs on the other important players. He does not seem like the man to turn away from his woman."

"I would have said the same," I said. "And maybe there was a Hider working their magic on me." Something I hadn't had a chance to mull over. I changed directions. "I tell you that because in the facility, they were keeping us quiet with a form of mind control. Not one abnormal, with the exception of the Magelore, retained any special abilities. Myself included. I'm blocked off from anything I could do before." I mean, there was Cowboy, but he hadn't been able to use his EMP pulse, so maybe he'd lost that too.

Their eyes widened.

"You mean . . ." Carlos shook his head, "they took away your powers?"

"I think they buried them deep under some sort of false memory. They gave us new names and told us that all we'd lived before was a lie, a memory of lives that didn't exist. If you fought them, they hurt you. If you kept fighting them, they killed you."

"How did you survive?" Anita asked. "If they were so inside your mind?"

There was fear in her voice and it was not unwarranted.

"I gave them exactly what they wanted. I gave them compliance and agreement. I never took a step out of line after they stuck me in the facility. But they were still watching me, as you can see. And I'm sure they kept sedatives in the food. Which I ate. Because I had to."

"The last day?"

"I didn't eat as much. I claimed I wasn't feeling well." I pushed my plate away from me, feeling that same nausea. "They made it addictive, I'm sure."

"Oh," Anita said, "you are looking rather green."

I nodded and my stomach gurgled. I refused to throw up the first real meal I'd had in far too long. "I need to sleep."

"He fled to Europe," Carlos said as I stood. "With at least your son. There was no record of a girl."

Hope, dangerous and so desperately needed, flared in my chest. "Did they make it?"

"He made it there, but the purge spread. What started here, most of the world adopted." Carlos shook his head. "There is no safe place for us any longer."

His words hit me harder than I would have thought possible—or maybe it was the withdrawal from the drugs in my system—and I stumbled after Anita. She led me away from the dining room, and my dog followed.

"What is her name?"

"Hasn't got one yet," I said.

Anita held open a bedroom door. "It is my daughter's room, but she wouldn't mind. There is a bathroom attached and you can use any of her clothes you find."

She shut the door behind me, and I damn well knew she was trying to play on my sympathies. It wouldn't work. I wasn't looking for their daughter. I couldn't. Not if I was going to find my boy.

I forced myself into the bathroom and ran a hot shower. The heat was a welcome distraction and I hissed as the water hit the sore points on my body where the tracers still resided. "Like I've been hit with buckshot," I muttered, soaping up and scrubbing away the smell of the facility.

The dog gave a soft woof as I stepped out of the shower and toweled off. I ached all over, but the fatigue of a full belly, hot shower, freedom, and fear were crashing down on me and I fell onto the bed.

The dog jumped up and lay beside me and I slung an arm over her, an anchor in this storm I didn't quite know how I was going to get through.

Sleep caught me quickly and I didn't fight it, didn't try to navigate my mind, or the things I needed to keep away from those who would read my thoughts.

The current that had been swirling through me, hidden away, swept over my dreams and I found myself wandering in the darkness as if I were meditating.

"Bear!" I called my son's name, hoping but not expecting an answer.

"MOM!"

I spun to see him running toward me. His face was filthy as if he'd been rolling around in ashes, and his clothes were torn, but he was alive. I caught him in a hug, shocked at how much he'd grown. He was up to my shoulder now, too big to scoop up. Nearly fourteen, he'd lived more than most people did in fifty years.

He clung to me, sobs ripping out of him. "I knew you weren't dead. I knew you weren't dead."

The irony was not lost on me. This would not be the first time he'd been told I was dead only to find out that I wasn't.

"Don't tell me where you are," I said. "There may be people watching. Tell me if you are okay, if you are safe."

He tipped his face up to me and I marveled that he was there. Not once in all the times I'd checked in on him had I dared reach out to him. Even in my safe place, I'd worried about drawing attention to him.

"I . . ." He shook his head. "I have Captain with me." Captain was his dog, a Malinois like Abe had been. "The three of us are hiding."

Three.

"Killian?"

Bear bit his lower lip. "No. He disappeared a few weeks ago. Mom, he was just gone one day. I woke up and he was gone."

He would never voluntarily leave Bear during this madness. "Who is with you?"

"Just me and—" He turned his head. "I have to go. Mom, we're okay. We're safe right now."

"I'll check on you every night. I'm coming," I

whispered into his hair, kissing the top of his head as he faded away.

Gone, just like that.

Did I dare try to reach Killian?

"Fuck," I muttered and did a slow turn. "Killian, you sexy Irish asshole, where are you?"

I strode through the darkness and the fog, but there was no response from him. But if he was in a facility, and his mind was blanked out . . . my guts clenched, and I woke in a cold sweat.

What if Killian was trapped like I had been? No, that wasn't quite right. Eligor had never tried to control me to the extent the others had been controlled. Killian could be like Easter—his mind blank, his body working on autopilot. Or worse . . . if he'd fought them too hard, they might have killed him outright. I'd seen it happen to over a dozen abnormals at the facility, so it was more than plausible.

As much as I was angry that he'd let me be taken, that was not the reality. He wouldn't have just let me be taken.

He'd thought I was dead.

And now he could be the one on the cold side of the grave.

I fell out of the bed and barely made it to the toilet where I lost all that good food. I heaved until there was nothing left. Heaved until the sweat slid down my face.

I pressed my pounding head into my hands as I propped myself up on my elbows. My dog came and sat next to me, her one good eye watching me closely. There was no judgment there, she was just waiting.

Waiting for me to make a decision.

"Hey, girl." I dug my hands into the skin around her neck and scrubbed her fur, expecting her to close her one good eye in enjoyment as any other dog would.

She locked her gaze on mine and didn't look away. Her scarred ear twitched, then both flicked back and she let out a soft growl.

Not at me.

At whatever she was hearing inside the house.

I pushed to my feet and scrounged around Rosita's clothes, pulling on jeans that were on the loose side, a T-shirt, socks, and a pair of beat-up Adidas that were a shade big too. I scooped Dinah up from the bed.

"What's happening?" she asked.

"Dog is upset about something," I said.

I went to the bedroom door and slowly turned the handle, cracking it open. The clock beside the bed read three in the morning, so I'd only been out a few hours.

Voices, soft, hushed, urgent.

I slid out of the door and crept down the hall, dog at my heels. Her big paws were silent on the carpet.

"Are you sure, Carlos?" Anita whispered. "This is the *Phoenix* we're talking about."

I edged myself to the doorway so I could see them, but they couldn't see me.

"They took her once, she's not invulnerable." He rubbed a hand over his face. "And she wouldn't agree to look for Rosita. They could bring our girl back to us. It is a trade worth making."

A chill swept down my spine, and I had a very bad feeling I knew what was happening.

"You dosed the food good? I know we weren't sure if we would need it," he said.

"Yes." Anita shook her head. "I didn't think she was going to eat anything at first."

"I didn't either. The Magelore has agreed to help us pin her down." He took his wife's hands and I slid back down the hall.

Everyone had an angle, everyone had a reason for cutting your legs out from under you. So Peter wanted to do his own thing, did he? Fucking Magelores.

I crept back down the hall, not to my room, but to Cowboy's. I turned the knob and slid through, motioning for the dog to follow. When she did, I shut the door without a sound.

Tucking Dinah into my waistband, I went to

Cowboy and grabbed his shoulders. He didn't so much as move. Fuck, I couldn't carry him.

"We have to leave him," Dinah said. "We don't have a choice."

The door creaked open and I spun, grabbing Dinah and holding her steady on Peter as he stepped through. He held up both hands. "Don't shoot," he whispered.

The only reason I didn't was because I didn't want the two Hiders to know I was awake.

"They've phoned the facility," Peter said. "They want my help to pin you down. We have to go."

I narrowed my eyes and my finger rested heavily on the trigger. Dinah growled. "Fucking traitor."

Peter shook his head. "You can't get that kid out of here by yourself. I can pack him. You go get what you can from those two."

I didn't lower Dinah. "No double-crossing?"

"Well, I'm double-crossing them. But I know who the top dog is here, and I am sticking with her on this front." He tipped his head at the dog at my side.

"Funny," I muttered, and lowered Dinah, half expecting him to rush me. But he didn't. He moved slowly, as if he knew I was on edge, and stopped next to the bed, looking down at the kid.

"He's really got to get his legs under him. All this packing him around is getting old fast."

"Search the room, find a couple bags," I said as I

slipped out the door and headed to the other side of the home. I didn't bother to hide my steps.

Hiders were talented, but they didn't tend to be fighters. And I had no desire to kill abnormals— weird since that was exactly what my father had trained me to do.

Anita looked up as I stepped into the kitchen, but her eyes didn't go wide. They closed and her mouth whispered what I suspected was a prayer.

"Double-crossing me rarely goes well for anyone," I said softly, my voice even. The dog at my side let out a low growl, picking up on my anger even though I sounded as if I were about to thank them for their hospitality.

Carlos put both hands on the round kitchen table and stared down the hall. I waited as Peter came up beside me, the kid slung over his shoulder. "Sorry, my friend, I'm with the mean one. She'll survive this, if anyone can."

He tossed a couple of empty bags out onto the dining room table.

"Money. Weapons. Easy food," I said. "Fill it, Anita. Peter, go with her. Make sure no more phone calls are made."

She opened her eyes and took in the bags. "We just want our daughter back."

I slammed my hand against the table, making them both jump. "You think I don't want my kid back? You think I don't want to stop whatever the fuck is going on here? Who else is going to do it? The strong ones are *gone!* Who else is left? WHO? You called them down on me, the *one person left* who might have a fucking chance to see this through!" I was yelling and I didn't care.

The words were out of my mouth, driven by my anger, before I could catch them. I hadn't even realized that part of me *had* thought about stopping this.

"Wait, you're going after them?" Peter sounded as shocked as Carlos and Anita looked.

Every muscle in me tightened. "No. That was not what I meant."

"Sure sounded like it was what you meant," Dinah muttered.

"It's not," I said. The mother bear in me wanted only to find my boy, to hold him in real life and not in a vision, and then spirit both of us away from the danger. I could do it. I knew I could hide us both.

Even without your abilities?

That was my own voice inside my head, not the one that had spent the past year in my skull, but I still shivered.

"They would find you, eventually. And that wouldn't protect your son." Carlos slumped into a chair. "Trust me, if I couldn't keep my daughter safe, you don't have a chance with your boy, no matter how much you love him." His eyes locked on mine, forcing me to hear him out. "If what you say about the facilities is true, your son would end up somewhere just like Clearview, his mind wiped blank, his body nothing more than a shell. Or dead. I suppose that might be better in a way."

I let rage pool in my eyes, washing away any emotion. "Then I suppose you are hoping that your daughter is dead?"

Anita gasped. "No."

Carlos, though, nodded. "Yes. Better for her to be gone than to be a blank, a nothing."

Bear . . . dead . . . or a blank, which was worse? Shivers ran through my body and my skin flushed hot. "How long before they're here? The facility?"

"We didn't call them yet," Anita whispered. "We . . . weren't sure."

Behind me Peter slumped. "Jesus. I'm going back to bed."

"Wait," Carlos said. "She is the only one left, Magelore. Despite what you are, you are no Vivian."

Vivian had been a legend in Magelore circles, old, strong, mean as a snake with a kink in its tail, and I'd killed her when she'd teamed up with my father.

Peter grunted. "Wouldn't want to be that. But you're right, I'm not as strong as Viv. You aren't going to convince her." He pointed a thumb at me. "She's not got emotions you can manipulate like a normal person."

Carlos and Anita shared a look. "What if . . . what if I offered to come with you?" he said. "I will be your personal Hider. You'll move in shadows."

I looked at him, seeing a genuine desire in his face. "If I'll go after the big bad uglies? That's the deal?"

"None of us are safe," Carlos said, not begging but close. "Not you, not me, not our children, until this force that has decided to wipe us out has been dealt with. Phoenix, you could be that person."

He was persistent, I'd give him that.

Anita was just as dogged. "Someone has to stand up against these monsters."

I turned my gaze on her. "I'm the biggest monster of all, Anita. And I couldn't do it. They caught me, kept me penned up, and it was a stroke of fucking *luck* that got us out of there. Even with a Hider it would be . . ."

No, I wasn't even going to consider this route. I'd left Bear behind so I could tackle the beast that was my father. And I'd nearly lost my son.

I wouldn't take that gamble again.

Peter cleared his throat. "Nobody else has had luck like that. And from what the kid said, there are other facilities that have as many or more abnormals trapped."

Carlos and I stood across from each other while Peter talked me up. "Why do you care, Magelore?"

He looked to the floor. "I have a penance to pay. Something I shouldn't have done, but did anyway, believing that I would be safe. I was a fool to help them."

I sucked in a slow breath, understanding dawning, but it was Dinah who called him out.

"You motherfucking goat's ass! You sold us out? You did, didn't you?" She squirmed in my hand, trying to tip her barrel at him, but I deliberately kept her pointed at the floor.

She didn't mean me in particular, or even her, but the collective us. The abnormals he'd helped them hunt down.

Peter didn't lift his head. "I thought they were going to be like the mob bosses. I figured I was throwing my lot in with the strongest kid on the block." Slowly he raised his head. "But I was wrong. As soon as they were done with me, they tossed me in the basement and left me to rot."

I could have shot him right there and been done with it but there was something he had that we needed. "You have information about them then?"

He swallowed hard. "Some. They didn't give me much, but I'll tell you everything I know."

Everything he knew turned out to be far more than he'd been letting on.

12

"WE HAVE TIME," ANITA SAID AS THE FOUR OF US SAT at the dining room table. "Our abilities will keep us hidden until morning. Even with our address, they won't be able to find the house."

"That seems awfully generous," I said. They might be Hiders, adept at slipping through the cracks, but I'd been on the run before, and twelve hours was a long time to sit in one place. My dog dropped her head onto my lap, her one eye locked on me. As if she knew I was on the verge of bolting.

Carlos ran his hands over his head. "We have run into similar problems before. We have a good amount of time."

I wasn't sure I bought that. "We'll count on six hours, tops."

Which meant we had maybe two left before they came knocking. Peter tapped on the table.

"Here's the deal. They hired me to identify any abnormals they brought in. Type, abilities, strength, that sort of stuff. I can tell from the tiniest drop of blood. They were supposed to repay me with my freedom."

Of course, they'd drawn blood from all of us. And fed it to a fucking Magelore.

"Did they have another Magelore for the other facilities?" I asked, ignoring the look of hope on Anita's face. I wasn't asking because I was going to do this. I was asking because it was smart to know what your enemy was up to.

"Far as I know, yes. Though who is anyone's guess. I do know there are at least two other facilities." He looked up at the ceiling and closed his eyes. "Eligor—I knew him as Ernest—was kind of the boss of the little handlers. The ones who got in your heads. The big boss back at the facility is Gardreel. He is . . . something else, but I couldn't tell—"

"Demon," I said, thinking about my one look at Gardreel and the way the wind moved his long red coat when there was no wind. "They are demons."

Only Peter was already shaking his head. "No. I've run into demons before. They are not those."

"Eligor is a demon name," I said. "And I'd bet anything Gardreel is a demonic name too."

Peter frowned. "I didn't taste them, so I could be wrong, but they don't act like demons, Nix."

"What do they act like?" Dinah asked.

The Magelore drummed his fingers across the table. "Like they were doing something good? Like they had a higher calling? They kept me in the dark for the most part, so a lot of this is conjecture. But the word 'cleanse' came up more than once. They want all the abnormals gone. Humanity restored."

Anita and Carlos shared a look that spoke volumes.

"What?"

"Our daughter, she said something about the people running these places. She managed to speak to one of them here, at the Clearview Rehabilitation Center with her partner. She said that they weren't like anything she'd tangled with before. They acted like they were better than everyone else," Carlos said. "Could this be a new kind of abnormal? One we haven't seen before?"

Cleansed. Higher calling. New abnormals. Demonic names.

Had they taken the names of demons out of a sense of irony? I didn't think so.

"Do you have a VPN on your computer?" I asked. "I need to look something up."

"Yes, our daughter did that for us, another way to keep our tracks clear." Anita stood and motioned for me to follow her. I tucked Dinah into the waistband of my pants and she mumbled something about being cocky and putting her away before I knew it was safe.

Anita led me to a room with a tiny window and a nice shiny new computer all set up. She logged in and I sat.

Working off a search engine, I put in Eligor's name first. It came up under a list of demon names, just like I'd thought it would. I scrolled down, seeing more names I recognized from my previous research on demons.

"Something isn't adding up," I said. I typed in "demons" and "higher calling" on a whim. A whim that paid off.

What came up under the search made me sit back, and Anita gasped. "Madre de dios. Is that possible?"

Yeah, pretty much my question too.

I did a few more searches, refining the wording until I knew I was on the right track.

Finally, I sat back in the chair. Fewer than fifteen minutes had passed, but I had my answer. I didn't like it, not one bit.

Suddenly I wasn't so sure that I could just walk away from this mess. I leaned over the small computer table, gripping the edges. A hand settled gently on my back. "Breathe."

Normally I'd have thrown off the hand and the

suggestion, but fear and anger were strangling me. Fear for my son. Rage that I was going to . . . deal with this when all I wanted was to see him. Hold him. Breathe him in. This was not the life I'd chosen. I'd walked away from it—twice now.

And yet . . .

"Zee . . . he was a good man, and the best Hider I ever met." The warmth of her hand sank into my back. "He told me once that he was training a girl who moved and hunted like a jungle cat with no remorse for her prey. But that if she loved you, she fought for you more fiercely than anyone he'd ever seen. That underneath all the death was a fire that burned bright and clean for justice."

She stood there, her hand on me. "If you want your son to be safe, there is only one answer. Because these creatures will find you no matter where you go. You know what you must do."

And then she stood and left me in that little room, a cold spot where her palm had been resting, her words hammering at me.

"Goddamn it!" I snapped out the words and the table cracked under the pressure of my fingers. "Dinah?"

"Yeah, she's good," she said carefully. "But that's not what you're asking, is it?"

I closed my eyes as the tears formed. Tears of

rage, of pain, of all the emotions I couldn't indulge in. "I can't . . . I can't leave him behind again."

"But are you leaving him behind?" she asked. "Or are you protecting him? That's the question."

I slowly released the table under my fingers and made myself type in a few more key searches. Nothing came up on how to deal with these fuckers. How to kill them. How to stop them.

"You going to tell me what's on the screen?" Dinah asked. "I can only see so far when I'm stuffed into your pants."

I turned the computer off and headed back to the dining room, my body cold from what I'd seen. From what I was already committing to do.

I'm so sorry, Bear. I'm so sorry that I'm not coming for you.

Four abnormals waited for me, Cowboy finally awake and sitting upright. Sort of. He was slumped in his chair, his eyes foggy from the drugs in the dinner.

"It's worse than you could possibly imagine," I said, not sitting.

Peter's face paled. "That is not cool, Nix, coming out of your mouth."

I folded my arms. "The names—Eligor and Gardreel—they are demonic names in some circles, but in others . . . they are the names of the fallen.

Angels who either chose to leave their realm or were kicked out for a variety of reasons."

I'd basically dropped a bomb on the middle of the table. Dinah was the first to speak, eloquent as always. "What the fuck? So fallen angels that act like demons? Feathers and shit?"

"No feathers that I saw," Peter said.

They were all looking at me, and I held each of their gazes in turn, ice forming over my heart. I had to put it away for a little longer.

"I have an idea. But we need to move and quickly, because if there are angels—fallen or otherwise—looking for us, then I have no doubt they have the ability to track us."

Anita gave me a sad, hopeful smile. "Then you will try to stop them?"

"On one condition," I said.

"Anything," she whispered, and because she was a mother too, I suspected she already knew.

"You will find my boy, and you will hide him until I can get to him," I said.

She gave a slow nod. "He'll be in Europe."

"Start looking in Ireland." As soon as I said it out loud, I wanted to take it back, despite knowing two Hiders were using their skills to keep us as hidden as anyone could be. "What's left of the Irish mobsters will have the latest info. When you find him . . . tell him that Montana is pretty in summer, but a wintry bitch." That was our code phrase.

Anita hurried from the room. "I'm leaving now for the airport." As she passed me, she reached out and touched my arm. "On my life and the life of my own child, I will protect him."

I didn't like the way my throat tightened. It should have been me leaving, not her. "Tell him I'll be there soon."

She bobbed her head and then she disappeared deeper into the house. I knew she would pack weapons, using her ability to hide them from the TSA agents. Fifteen minutes later, she was gone, down the road and on her way to Bear. I didn't have a picture of him, but I'd described him as best I could.

"I met your father once," Anita had said. "I'll recognize your boy if he favors your side so strongly."

Just me and the boys left—and, of course, Dinah.

They'd packed their bags too, and the room was quiet.

"What are we waiting for?" Cowboy asked.

The gray dog hadn't left my side through all this, standing with me. Feeling my pain. She let out a low whine and I dropped my right hand to her head, the touch soothing her and me. "We need a plan. They're going to find us, but if we're smart, we'll take them on a road trip."

I explained what I was thinking, the plan spilling out of me.

Cowboy liked it.

Carlos was hesitant and Peter . . . well, Peter didn't like it one bit.

"I'm not bait!" he snapped. "I'm a fucking Magelore! I may not be as feared as you, but I'm no chump change to be used as petty BAIT!"

I raised an eyebrow. "They aren't going to catch you. I'm sending Carlos with you, remember? When the moment comes, he'll hide you both, and then you'll meet back up with me and Cowboy."

Peter's jaw ticked and danced with irritation. "Fuck." Just like that, he'd agreed.

Carlos cleared his throat. "Before we go on, I must apologize for even thinking of handing you over. The stories about you—"

"Are true," I said. "But that is what makes me uniquely designed to kill every single one of these fuckers and burn their world to the ground without flinching." Eligor would have been the only one I left alive, but he was gone. Terminated.

He tipped his head at me. "I have something you should take."

He led me down the hall into the last bedroom, the master suite. Done up in floral blues and greens, the room was probably meant to be soothing, yet I felt nothing but a pulse of anxiety. Was this how the rest of the world tried to sleep?

"Help me push the bed," he said. I bent next to him and shoved the bed, scratching the hardwood. The floor beneath the bed didn't look any different, but he waved his hand over a section of it and an iron pull appeared. Hiders. Sneaky bastards. He grabbed the ring and opened a small space, three feet by three feet, maybe a bit bigger.

"I have a weapon here, like yours. He's a mouthy thing, but I think he will help you. He loves Anita like a sister," Carlos said.

Dinah shivered. "A sentient gun? Like me?"

I grabbed him by the shoulder and dragged him back. While he was theoretically on my side, I couldn't risk letting him pull a gun. If he attacked me, I'd have to shoot him, and we still needed him.

Keeping him on my right, I reached into the darkness, and my fingers brushed against the metal butt of what felt like a larger gun. Something semi-automatic by the feel of it.

A voice breathed out of the small space. "Oh, baby, just like that. Carlos, you didn't tell me that you were giving me to a pretty girl!"

I raised an eyebrow at Carlos. "It's no small thing to have a sentient gun. I thought I had the only two."

He shrugged. "He was a ladies' man in life. That

didn't change after. And it was his wish to be . . . placed in a gun to protect someone he loved."

I was going to have a longer chat with Dinah about the spell used on her. Find out just how many people knew about it.

"Hey, Carlos, you fucker, you going to let me go do some damage?" the gun yelled as I dragged him out of the hiding spot.

He was no handgun, but an AK-47, with what looked like a seriously long-range scope. Matte black —he had that much in common with Dinah. I rolled him over once. "What's your name?"

He shivered in my hands. "Well, that depends. You want the name I was born with?"

"I need a name so I can yell at you," I said.

He chuckled. "A woman with fire? Bring it on, baby. You can call me Diego."

Carlos cleared his throat. "We should go. We have less than thirty minutes before they arrive."

I looked at him as the rumble of an engine cut through the walls of the house, soft, barely there but I heard it. My dog lifted her head and I turned toward the front of the house.

"Correction, we are out of time."

13

I gave Carlos one last look as the engines of what sounded like three distinct army trucks rolled up the driveway to his house. "You did call them."

He grimaced. "It was the deal. I'm sorry, I—"

"Don't be sorry, get your fucking keys and get ready to move. I don't want you in the line of fire."

He was like a goose that laid golden eggs; a Hider in this world where we were about to be on the run could be the difference between our survival and death.

I held the new gun, Diego, up and settled his stock against my shoulder. "What can you do, boyo?" That was the bit of Killian I carried with me coming out. Boyo.

Diego gave a happy chuffing sound. "The usual. Exploding rounds, rapid fire, distance shots, whatever you need. But I want a certain number of kills, you hear?" he said. "Oh, and I can shift to a more manageable size too, if I get to be too big for your tiny girly hands."

"He's from the Bronx," Dinah said. "I can hear it in his voice. And she does not have tiny hands. Idiot."

"I am not from the Bronx," Diego said. "If I'm from the Bronx, you're from jolly old England, sass mouth."

They quarreled back and forth as I checked the hidden storage box and pulled out a strap that would keep the new gun slung over my shoulder and back, plus a box of what I hoped was extra special ammo. A leather belt that had a holster went around my waist.

"Welcome to the crew. You'll have your share of blood."

"Fucking right," he growled. "I like that you aren't running. Stand your ground, mess the bastards up."

Dinah sighed and then laughed. "He's going to have to learn that he's second string. I get first blood."

"Not tonight."

I tucked her into the holster and she squawked. "What the fuck?"

I swept Diego around and went to the window.

The trucks in the driveaway had parked and men were spilling out of them, crouched low as they scuttled toward the house. "Peter, in here!"

The Magelore appeared at my side as if by magic. "We really going to fight?"

"They don't know we're awake. They didn't even send a full crew." I motioned at the thirty or so men in tactical wear who were creeping forward and circling the house. "I want the goodies in that truck. Weapons, gear, information. I want it all. And then we're going to ram it up their asses."

The big gun shivered in my hands. "Oh yeah, talk dirty to me, baby." He said baby like bay-bay with just the slightest hint of an accent.

Peter glanced at me. "New gun?"

"Yup." I stepped forward and quietly slid the bedroom window open, dropped to my knees, and lifted the gun. "You got a silencer?"

"I do," Dinah grumbled.

"Nope," Diego said.

That was that. "Peter, you want to eat?"

"Seriously?"

I didn't even look at him. "If you want a meal, this is your chance. Fill up on them. I've got you covered."

He was gone before I took another breath. I didn't wait to see him stalking his prey but got things going on my end of the fight.

I squeezed the trigger on the new gun and the guy in front of the approaching group went flying backward from the force of the bullet slamming into his forehead.

Pop, pop, pop. Rapid fire was handy, and I used it to our advantage, mowing down the first wave of soldiers headed our way. Humans for sure, they didn't get back up. Fifteen down. The other fifteen or so scattered, looking for cover. I picked them off as they ran. Two more on the left, four on the right.

Nine left. This was going well. About as good as I could have hoped.

My dog lay at my feet, not moving an inch even with all the gunfire. Her ears lay flat against her head and I could feel her emotions. She wanted to fight. That was what she'd been trained for. To sink her teeth into flesh.

"Better hurry, Peter!" I yelled.

The Magelore launched out of the darkness and took two soldiers down at once, rolling across the ground with them. My stomach turned and I struggled not to turn the gun on him. But if I was going to have him with me, he needed to feed regularly. Which meant I needed to ensure it happened.

"Exploding rounds," I said and the inner workings of the gun gave a click. I fired on two soldiers lifting their guns toward Peter and his prey. The new bullets hit them and their tactical gear shredded; they fell back screaming.

"I wanna see!" Dinah whined. "And I wanna shoot something!"

"You'll get your chance, but I have to see what Diego can do, and if he's worth taking with us," I said.

"What the fuck? I'm the best you'll ever have, baby," he growled.

"Heard that before," Dinah said. "Usually two minutes before they groan and say they're done."

I couldn't help it, my lips twitched. "You know, Dinah, you're right about that. No stamina these days."

"WHAT?" Diego yelped as I ducked below the window. "I'll show you two ladies what you've been missing!"

Return fire was on us now, the humans finally pulling their shit together and taking out the glass above, sending it all over the room like sharp confetti. I dropped and slid backward, crawling across the floor to the hall, the dog following on her belly. Once there, I stood and headed back to the dining room, snapping my fingers for her to keep up. Silently she kept pace at my side. The door in that room was a glass slider, open about ten inches to let the night air in. I kept Diego raised as I swept toward the backyard and stepped out into the cool air of the night.

Screaming ripped through the silence, then cut off.

Peter was done feeding.

I picked up my pace. We needed to move. There would be backup coming as soon as someone got smart and radioed in that they were in trouble.

Movement to my left swung me in that direction and I squeezed off a round at close range. The soldier's face exploded, bone and bits of his helmet spraying in every direction.

"Booyah!" Diego yelped. "That was a good one. I didn't even see him!"

I kept moving, not bothering to wipe the blood and bits of the soldier's brains from my skin. By my count, we had a half-dozen soldiers left scattered about. Should have been easy, but the prickling of my skin said we had more to worry about than a few humans with guns.

A knife slashed at me from the darkness, and I stepped back, the blade just missing my face. Another step, and another as the blade kept swinging. "You killed my friend!"

"Oh dear," Dinah said. "You should not bring a knife to a gun fight."

I yanked her clear and shot him point blank as he

brought the knife down. It cut across my arm, but the strike lost momentum as he died and fell to the side.

I tucked her back into the holster. "Happy?"

"It was a good line," she said. "I've been waiting to use it."

Another time, I would have rolled my eyes, but the job wasn't done. My dog gave a low rumbling growl as we cleared the side of the house. That was how I felt too, but there were no soldiers standing and Peter was the only one I saw.

Danger screamed through my body, making my skin prickle, hair standing at attention along the back of my neck and arms. Peter grinned at me, but I shook my head. "Something's wrong."

His grin faded and I moved carefully toward the big army vehicle that had brought the soldiers.

Soldiers who had died easily.

Soldiers who had kept us pinned down for the last ten minutes.

"Fuck," I whispered the word as I swept the area, searching for what was coming. My dog butted her head against my thigh and gave a low whine. I glanced at her and saw she wasn't looking at me.

She was looking straight up.

I looked up with her.

"Peter. What kind of abnormal flies with wings?"

"None that I know of—Jesus Christ, what are those?"

Which was what I'd thought he'd say, because I was with him on this. I knew all the abnormals out there, that was part of the job I'd had. I'd never once heard or seen anything like what was coming at us. Which meant they weren't abnormals. They were something else.

They were the fallen.

Three creatures dropped from the sky, leathery wings spread wide, bringing the stench of death and rot with them. They landed as a trio, hard enough to dent the concrete and send a ripple out toward us. Each one had four arms, foot-long claws dangling from their hands, and legs that looked like tree trunks bent at odd angles, like a horse's back legs. Their mid-sections rippled with muscle, but their faces looked human, and even had a vestige of beauty that made it seem as if their heads had been photoshopped onto their incredibly monstrous bodies.

"Dinah, you're going to get your wish." I pulled her from her holster and tossed her to Peter.

"Jesus," he muttered again as the creatures rose on their strange legs, easily ten feet tall, and started toward us.

"Not Jesus," I said softly. "Fallen angels. Incendiary rounds."

The trio tucked their wings back, but didn't slow

their pace, as if they didn't care that we had guns trained on them.

"I don't have incendiary rounds," Diego said.

"Fuck. Keep it exploding then." I spoke as I squeezed off the first round. The bullets hit the fallen one on the far left of us, and while it rocked him backward, there was no real wound. No blood, and the creature didn't even slow his approach. "Something else, what else have you got?" I yelled as I kept firing.

I aimed for the joints in the legs, hoping the force of the bullets would at least knock the ugly fuckers down.

Peter squeezed off a few of Dinah's fiery rounds, and that seemed to drive the creatures back. For a moment. And then they stepped over the flames and kept on coming.

I caught one in the knee, and the joint dislocated, the big ugly going down with a howl. His two buddies looked at him. "Get up," the one in the middle said. "For the glory of the creator, get up and abolish this filth."

"Look who's talking! You might as well have crawled out of a goat's ass, stinking like shit and saying a field of daisies smells bad!" Dinah yelled in between shots. She had a knack for the insults, I'd give her that.

The one I'd downed tried to get back up, but I

kept working on those joints, snapping them with the force of the bullets even if they weren't actually doing permanent damage. I backed up and aimed at the knees of the one closing in on Peter.

The creature whipped a wing around and blocked the bullets. They bounced off the wing as if it were metal.

What the actual fuck was happening here?

I swung the gun around on its strap and charged the creature. His eyes widened and he swept one of his four arms toward me. I grabbed him by the hand and reversed direction, snapping his arm with my entire body weight. The crack of bone filled the air, but I didn't stop. I spun, still hanging onto his arm, so I twisted it completely free of all attachments with the exception of his skin.

He roared and another arm came for me. I let go and went low, kicking at his knees, knocking him sideways.

"For big, monstrously ugly motherfuckers, you sure aren't all that scary," I said. No doubt they were used as the final intimidation once the soldiers had pinned down the abnormals they were hunting.

The one in the middle shot toward me—and I mean shot. He was standing still one moment and the next I had all four of his hands on me, holding me by the arms and legs, stretched out.

My dog snarled and leapt forward, grabbing him

around the ankle and tearing him from side to side. She didn't put a dent in him, but at least she kept him off balance.

"We have you now." He smiled and his face lit up.

"Shock her," said the one who seemed to be the leader.

"Nix!" Dinah yelled. The lights around us dimmed, the streetlights popping and the world going completely dark as the creature holding me lit up like a fucking mini-sun. He was clearly drawing all that power into him. This was going to hurt like a motherfucker, no matter how I looked at it.

"Ruby," the dog's name came to me in that moment, "release!" I yelled as my limbs were pulled taut, muscles straining. Ruby backed off, but she was whining and growling, her body hunched as she stalked around the freakish creature that held me tightly.

I didn't fight the power as it slammed into me, designed to maim and kill.

I welcomed it.

14

THE SURGE OF POWER SNAPPED MY TEETH SHUT AND I closed my eyes to keep them from bugging out of my head. Breathing was not an option as the jolt surged through me three times, cutting into my head, lighting up my nerve endings. I fought to hold onto it, pooling all that power in my lower back—strange, I know, but that was where I'd kept stuff like this before.

Killian's ability was one of lightning and I could absorb his power and hold it in order to discharge it at my leisure later. I was hoping this would be the same. I was hoping I wasn't completely blocked from this ability the way Cowboy was from his EMP pulse.

That's the thing with being an abnormal. We were all different, even the ones with similar abilities. Part of mine was being able to hang onto another form of energy and then redistribute it through a weapon. Usually Dinah.

Seeing as she was with Peter, Diego was about to get the shock of his afterlife. I hoped.

As quickly as it started, it was over.

The creature dropped me to the ground. "There. She is out."

I stayed down on the cold concrete, breathing hard, my eyes closed as I tried to feel my body.

As I tried to find my way through the blocks that had been put on me. They were still there, still holding me back.

Sweat rolled down my spine as I lay there unsure of how to untangle my abilities, so I could use the power that these fucking fallen had run through me.

The briefest touch of something in my mind kept me still. What felt like Eligor's fingers spread through my head and deftly unblocked the wall that kept me from my power, more carefully than I'd ever felt him move through my consciousness before. Smoother and . . . softer, almost gentle.

I didn't know how. I didn't know why, and I wasn't about to ask in that moment.

It was a weapon offered freely, and I was going to use it.

I opened my eyes.

"She's not out!" one of the fallen yelled, but I was already rolling onto my back and lifting Diego to my shoulder. They hadn't even bothered to take him from me. Cocky featherbrains.

I tapped into that power I'd pooled in my lower spine and sent it back *through my body*, down my arms and into the weapon as I squeezed the trigger. Just like I'd done in the past with the electricity Killian could manipulate and create.

The explosion that ripped out of Diego bashed into my eardrums, numbing my senses. This was more than just electricity, but a pure bolt of power I couldn't understand in all its strength.

The blow hit the creature in the chest and lit him up from the inside, showing his skeleton like a super-powered X-ray machine. His back arched and his wings went wide as he basically turned into a living breathing spotlight, the power tracing blood vessels, showing his heart beat and every tiny part of him.

I scrambled backward, still on my butt, and kept my weapon trained on him. There was no looking away, not for any of us, as his body began to shift and change. The leather skin of his wings sprouted feathers, his extra set of arms absorbed back into his body leaving him with only two, and his legs smoothed out and became strong, sleek limbs that any woman would want to dry hump like her life depended on it.

"Oh," Dinah said. "I'd bang him like a screen door."

Everything about the monster had shifted to a beauty so stunning that there was no earthly comparison for it. He slowly lowered to the ground and went to one knee, his back muscles rippling and trembling as his wings stretched wide. Fallen angel indeed.

He lifted a perfectly formed hand, his broad white-feathered wings dusting the ground. "How is this possible?"

Even his voice was beautiful, but no one had a chance to answer him.

A crack rent the air and the ground opened under him, red light spilling out. More hands than I could count reached up and pulled him into the crack, wrenching him into a space that was far too small for his large body and wingspan. Feathers burst up around him as those beautiful wings were shattered, ripped apart between the hands and the small space.

He screamed, reaching for his buddies, but they were already flying away.

Gone.

I blinked and the crack closed rapidly even as I stared at it until all that was left was a pile of white feathers. Silence ruled the world for a good ten seconds before car alarms started going off all the way up and down the street, and the neighborhood dogs began howling. Ruby bumped her head against my shoulder and gave a low growl as we stared at the still-smoking crack, but that was it from her.

"What the actual fuck just happened?" Peter stood next to me and reached a hand out. I took it and he helped me to my feet.

I swallowed hard, my throat dry and tight from all that power running through me. I had no answer, but a fearful possibility had begun to form inside my head.

The crack in the ground, the hands drawing the fallen down . . .

"Raid the truck," I said, my voice growly.

We moved fast. Cowboy and Carlos helped, silent. I didn't know how much they'd seen. What I knew was that my energy was going down the drain fast. I gritted my teeth and stumbled through the truck as I did a last check for needed items. Four bags of gear, tactical wear, walkie-talkies, anything we thought we could use. Including a tablet. I touched it and it lit up.

Clearview Rehabilitation Center.

I grabbed it and stuffed it under my shirt.

We stumbled out under the weight of the gear.

"Here," Carlos opened his garage and his four-door truck waited. "Throw it all in the back."

We did, and for a moment, I thought about letting Ruby get into the back too. Forget it. I took the front passenger seat and she climbed in with me, sitting at my feet. I tapped my lap and she climbed up, all sixty pounds of lean muscle, curling up like she was a lap dog. She let out a contented sigh. "Fierce, guard," I mumbled, trusting her to keep me safe as I leaned my head back. "Head north."

And just like that I was out cold.

Whatever had happened with the energy exchange was different from what I'd done before with Killian. With him, the electrical charge had left me feeling pumped, ready to fight, and full of energy I could barely contain. There had been no downside. But this . . . if someone had come at us right then, I would have been next to useless. I had no strength left in me. I couldn't even stay awake, never mind fight.

I slept for a few hours, truly slept, with no dreams of Bear, no walking through the foggy darkness of my sanctuary. When I woke, we were still on the road, heading north like I'd indicated before passing out.

Ruby was on my lap, snoring through her slightly flapping lips. Peter drove; Carlos and Cowboy were quiet in the backseats. The kid was out cold, but Carlos was awake.

"That dog of yours just rushed in there to help you." Peter shook his head. "You gave her a name?"

"Ruby," I said. "She's a gem."

She gave him a look with her one eye and a soft

woof. He shook his head. "Never had a dog like me before. They always know what I am." He reached over and touched her on the head with one finger. She gave him her one-eyed stink eye and licked his hand.

"What are we going to do with the kid?" Peter said. "He's not a bad one, but, Jesus. He's like a puppy too big for his own feet stumbling and tripping over himself."

"The plan hasn't changed. He'll come with me," I said.

Peter didn't answer. Carlos tapped the back of my seat. "The kid's abilities are strong, if untrained. And the fact that he avoided capture for so long says something, don't you think? I don't know if he'll be able to use his EMP pulse, but he's worth keeping. I agree."

I agreed with Carlos about Cowboy not getting snagged for a long time. In fact, it almost made me wonder if he was a plant. My jaw ticked and I forced the thought away. There was no way the facility and its overseers could have known I would make it out, or that I would attempt a breakout on that day. Hell, I hadn't known until moments before. They would have stopped me if they'd known.

Thinking of them, my head went to Eligor and the feel of him in my mind. He'd unbound my abilities just in time, and while he had been the one to help cage me, he'd saved me too. But had it been Eligor? That sensation was almost like him, but different enough that I noticed it.

For just a moment, I saw him, and he looked back at me. Only he wasn't the Eligor of before. This time he was a lanky, bespectacled college-looking guy. Fear was written all over his face. He shook his head, possibly as a warning, then was gone.

Fuck. They'd stuffed him in another body?

And we really were still connected. Could he keep them off me? Would he keep helping or would he end up turning on me too? Yeah, *fuck* was too weak a word for this.

"Sleeping Beauty!" Dinah cat-called with a whistle as Cowboy stirred. "Wakey, wakey, eggs and bakey!"

Peter went right to teasing Cowboy about missing out on all the action, watching it all as a spectator. Cowboy mumbled something about a Magelore and a sheep on a dark night, and Peter howled with laughter, though I didn't think it had been meant as a joke. Carlos smiled and shook his head, the fatherly figure in all this.

I put a hand over the assault weapon on my lap next to Dinah.

"Show me your smaller size."

He shivered. "Say please."

Dinah sighed. "Oh, don't be a shit. Do it."

"Please," I said though I wanted to throw him out the window for being an ass.

The gun clicked as though there were dozens of hidden gears inside of him, more than those needed for the firing of bullets. The AK-47 effectively shrunk to a weapon that could be hidden under a coat. A miniature AK-47. Not as small as Dinah, but I could put him on my back with a coat over top.

"I can shoot longer distances better full-sized, but pretty much everything else is the same," Diego said. "That work?"

"Good." I urged Ruby off my lap, then checked the two guns for damage and used the refills I'd snagged from Carlos's hidey-hole. After refilling the incendiary and smoke bomb rounds on Dinah, I flipped through the other ammo in the box. Most of it was simple stuff. Sedative rounds were new to me and could be useful. I poured the liquid into Diego's barrel.

Yes, it was just that simple with the guns.

"Think we might be needing to knock people out instead of kill them?" he asked.

"If we go up against another abnormal working under the influence of the handlers, I'd at least try to knock them out," I said, thinking of Easter. When I'd gotten that glimpse of Eligor, I thought I'd seen a flash of red hair behind him. It would not surprise me in the least if they used Easter to track us, and potentially kill me.

Peter cleared his throat. "Are we going to talk about what happened? With the angel wings and the crack that looked like it led straight to Hell and all the hands sucking him down, the smell of sulfur?"

My jaw ticked and I stared out the window, thinking. "I'm not sure what there is to say. You about summed it up. It confirms what I already believed— we are not dealing with abnormals."

Carlos nodded slowly. "I'd thought you would be wrong, but it looks indeed as though we are dealing with a fallen angel or angels. The others were afraid when they saw their friend taken. And that you did it to him."

I put a hand to my head, realizing that I had a pounding headache. Could be the drugs from dinner or withdrawal from the sedatives, but I suspected it was mostly from the power surge rocketing through me. My fingers tingled just thinking about it.

"Yeah, but what does it mean?" Peter tapped his fingers on the steering wheel. "He couldn't possibly have been an angel, not with that ugly shit he had going on."

I wasn't so sure. "Demons can make themselves look beautiful, and they usually do to fool the unwary and draw them into deals that can't be broken. They come in all shapes and sizes—"

"Like Eligor," Cowboy said. I nodded and went on. Because we weren't dealing with demons, I was sure of it. "They don't like to be seen as monstrous unless you've broken your end of a contract. That's when the ugly comes out. But these three . . . they were monstrous from the start." I frowned. "I don't understand why shooting its own power back at it made it look angelic, much less why it was then pulled through the planes of existence into what, yes, Peter"—I looked at him—"was probably a glimpse into Hell. Or a hellish plane, however you want to look at it."

Peter opened his mouth, flashing his fangs, and then shook his head. "But, wait, if you're right and these are fallen angels, what are they doing getting sucked down into Hell?"

I had an idea, but I was hoping I was wrong. "We need to get to a church. The info I need isn't going to be found in any database, book, or priest."

Cowboy leaned through the gap between the two front seats. "A church?"

"A particular church," I said quietly. "One that hosts a demon. And who better to tell us how to defeat a fallen angel than a demon?"

Cowboy's jaw dropped and he stuttered. "Are you insane? After that, you want to talk to a demon?"

Peter started laughing. "Is this what happens

when a thousand bolts of electricity zip through a person?"

"You two knob heads," Dinah said slowly, as if speaking to someone struggling to understand, "how many hunts and kills have you two ding-dong-alongs got between you? And I don't mean drink-down-your-dinner-too-fast kills, Magelore."

Diego laughed. "Oh, shit, who has been touching my butt exactly? Please, God, tell me she's as good as the Phoenix."

Dinah burst out laughing and I just kept my eyes on the road even though I wasn't driving. Neither Peter nor Cowboy could argue with Dinah, and they knew it. Carlos didn't even try. He'd worked with people like me in the dark underbelly of the world. People like his boss, Rio.

But like a lot of guys with too much testosterone and not enough thought process, the two younger guys believed they could do better than a trained professional. Fuck, they were going to cause me no end of grief.

A little niggling of something at the back of my neck told me it was time to split the group up. Instinct was a bitch and a blessing all in one.

I turned to Carlos. "How far have we gone from your place?"

He looked at the dash of the vehicle. "About a

hundred miles. Being safe with the posted speed limit, not drawing attention to us."

While it wasn't quite as far as I'd hoped we'd get, it would have to do.

"Pull over here." I pointed at a wide spot on the side of the highway. Peter did as I asked. I got out of the truck and Ruby followed, taking a sniff around the scrubby grasses on the side of the road.

"Carlos," I said as I grabbed two bags from the back of the truck and dragged them out, slinging them onto my back. My muscle strength and stamina weren't up to where I wanted them, but I'd get there. Ruby tucked in close to me. I pulled a leather strap out of one of the bags and made a quick collar and leash. She didn't need it, but appearances counted when it came to humans reporting you for stupid shit.

"Yes?" He didn't get out of the truck.

"You ready to play hide and seek?" I looked him in the eye. "Lead them as far to the west and north as you can. When they're on the wrong track and you're sure of it, hide both of you, then double back."

"This here is where we're splitting up?" Cowboy got out of the car, his blue eyes full of confusion. "We're not even in a town."

I glanced at him. "Those two are going to draw the eyes of the facility as far away as they can and everyone after us will expect a town stop if they figure out we've split up." I adjusted the bags in time to see a flash of hurt in his eyes. He thought I was leaving him behind.

"What about me?"

"Oh, you're special, sunshine," Peter said, and I realized from his tone he was more than a little jealous. "You get to go with the boss."

Cowboy took one of the bags from me, relief in his every move.

"I just don't want to wake up with you on top of me one night," I said to Peter. "You know, because then I'd have to kill you."

That made him laugh and the minor tension broke. I looked at Carlos. "You got it?"

"I got it. We'll meet you at the address in New York you gave me in three days."

I nodded. "I'll see what I can drum up between now and then."

Cowboy hefted his bag. "I'm glad I'm not going with him. No offense, Carlos. You seem cool enough."

Dinah sighed. "Oh good, because I really want to see what's in your pants."

Cowboy flushed. "I can listen, I can learn, I can help."

"Oh, for fuck's sake, he's got a hard-on for you. Take him and let him help," Peter yelled as he pulled away. "We'll draw them off, Phoenix, but don't you fucking forget to thank me in your speech at the end of all this. To the magnificent Magelore, Peter, for his noble sacrifice!" The last word was drawn out as he and Carlos sped onto the highway, leaving me there with Cowboy.

Diego grunted. "Heard his nickname for you. If they call you Phoenix, you must be a good killer."

"Did you not see her back there?" Dinah snapped. "She is the Phoenix. Not *like* the Phoenix, not *trained* by the Phoenix. The one and only."

Diego sucked in a breath. "Jesus. Tell me you're joking."

"She's not Jesus, she's Phoenix. Unplug your ears," Dinah snapped.

Standing on the highway was a good way to get noticed, especially with a dog, three massive army bags slung over our backs, and two sentient guns shouting your name. "Come on, this way." I headed straight for the light smattering of trees off the side of the interstate. Through the bush we went, doing our best not to create an obvious path.

"You'll train me?" Cowboy asked.

"Not in the sack!" Dinah squealed and then laughed.

"Why not in the sack?" Diego asked. "I'd take her training me in the sack. Probably rough, but I like a good spanking now and again."

Christ kill me now and leave me for dead, Dinah

had a friend to help torment me again. Though I'll admit this to no one, my lips might have twitched. Dinah sounded all but gleeful as the two of them went back and forth with all the positions I could show the young abnormal.

"Reverse cowboy, that will be his favorite!" Dinah hollered and Diego burst out laughing, the length of the gun shaking against my back.

Ruby trotted ahead of us, the makeshift leash dragging along through the bush as she sniffed her way along, her tail wagging here and there.

"She's happy," Cowboy said as if he could ignore the raunchy comments from the two guns. "I'm glad you brought her along."

I glanced at him, noting that he stared straight ahead, his face flushing pink off and on depending on what Dinah and Diego said. "She's a good girl. I've been feeding her the last month. I suspected they were going to put her down."

Cowboy did look at me then. "Like they would have put me and Peter down?"

I nodded. "I could see it in you from the first moment they dragged you in. There are some people who can't be broken. It's not a bad trait, but it'll get you killed in there."

"You weren't broken," he said.

"I bent," I replied and shrugged. "I figured out the tactics they would use real quick and gave them what they wanted. For some, it would be a pride issue. Their ego wouldn't allow them to be small, to be humble, to look broken." I stepped around a tree, avoiding a series of dried branches on the ground. He walked right through them. I shook my head. "My job is to survive, and that is your job too. You want me to train you, that is the first thing you need to know."

I could hear my mentor's voice in my head. Zee had been a survivor too, and he'd drilled it into me time and time again.

"Survive. No matter what you have to do, who you have to kill, what you have to agree to, you fucking survive. You can always make it better if you are alive. Can't do much from the grave."

I could almost feel Cowboy fighting that truth. "I don't want to—"

"Then you'll die," I said. "You don't have to like it, but it's the stone-cold truth. I'd tell my son the same thing." And in fact, I *had* told my boy that. I'd told him to fight when he could and run when he couldn't. There was no shame in living, but Zee was right about the last bit.

You couldn't make anything right if you were dead and buried.

This world was not survival of the fittest, but survival of the most adaptable.

We walked for maybe half an hour before we

came out at the top of an embankment that slid down into a sleepy suburb.

"You sure. . ." Cowboy cleared his throat and tried again. "What's the plan?"

"Good catch," Diego said. "You'll catch more flies with honey than vinegar."

I snorted. "And even more flies with shit." I paused while the two guns snickered. "The plan is to find another vehicle and head to New York."

"We don't have Carlos anymore. How are we going to get a vehicle without it being reported stolen?" he asked.

"Watch and learn, young grasshopper," I said as we stepped onto the main road that led through the suburb. We walked past more than half the houses on the street before I stopped and turned toward the domicile on our left. A house like all the others, painted blue with white shutters, a closed-in garage, gardens laid out along the edges. Very pretty, very suburban. Very quiet.

Cowboy kept up easily with his long legs and Ruby dropped to my side. I went to the back of the house and found what I was looking for. A small window at ground level. I gave it a kick, shattering it, then booted out the rest of the glass shards, making the opening clean and clear. I dropped the bags, took Diego off my back and handed him to Cowboy. "When you hear the car start up, come on around."

The light of the morning was changing, the early summer sun making itself known. We needed to be out of here before the rest of the suburbanites were awake and caffeinated enough to notice their neighbor's car being driven by a stranger.

I grabbed the top edge of the window and slid through, dropping silently to the floor. The stairs were right across from me and I jogged up them, not bothering to pull Dinah. There was no smell of abnormals here, and there was no way a powerful abnormal would live here. Well, unless they were a Hider like Carlos and Anita, in which case I wouldn't mind saying hello and having breakfast. But I doubted my luck was good enough for me to find another pair of Hiders so close to Carlos and Anita.

At the top of the stairs, I pushed the door open and slid through into the stale air of the rest of the house. Pamphlets lay all over the counter, and the helpful itinerary on the fridge informed me that Bob and Don wouldn't be back from their honeymoon until next week. They'd thanked Janice for taking care of their two cats.

Speaking of.

A sleek black cat with brilliant green eyes flounced into the room and flopped itself in front of me, stretching its legs out and pretty much pointing at the empty food dish, pushing it toward me with one paw. "Sorry, cat." I glanced at the list of instructions and found the black cat's name. Apparently she had a penchant for getting herself into trouble and the cat-sitter was to watch for that. "Zam. Pardon me, but I'm not the one feeding you."

A second cat, tawny with black points, strolled in, giving me a blue-eyed stare that said it all as it sat next to the first.

Feed us, slave.

"Fine. Be glad I left Ruby outside." I rummaged around, found their dry kibble, and topped up the dish.

"Happy?"

The black cat seemed to give me a wink and the tawny one bobbed his head. Cats. I'd never understand them. And these two were far too human for my liking.

I made my way into the bedroom and dug through the clothes until I found a pair of jeans and a T-shirt that looked to be close to Cowboy's size and threw the clothing over my arm.

Back in the kitchen, a set of keys hung from a brightly colored rainbow key hanger, and I scooped them off, heading for what would be the garage. The car waiting for me was a small import, dark blue with a leather interior and stick shift.

"Cute," I muttered. But it would do. I locked the garage door behind me and jammed it closed with a piece of pipe lying on the floor. Just in case Janice the house-sitter wanted to take their car for a spin. The longer we had without anyone noticing the car was missing, the better.

I slid into the driver's side and hit the button on the visor, opening the garage door. The engine started with no problem and I backed it out. Cowboy slung the three bags into the backseat of the car, and Ruby jumped on top of them, then rested her head on my shoulder from there.

Yeah, she was a good one. I hit the button, closing the garage as we pulled away. I tossed the clothes at Cowboy when he opened the door. "Change."

He slid into the passenger seat and managed to be quiet for all of three minutes as he wiggled out of his jeans and into the new clean ones. Brand name, no less.

We weren't out of the suburbs before he blurted out his question.

"How did you know to pick that place?" he asked. "How could you possibly know that was the best place to take a vehicle?"

I kept my eyes on the road, watching for any signs of pursuit as I worked my way back to the interstate and headed north again. I opened my mouth but then promptly snapped it shut on the answer.

"Hang on. We've got company."

15

THE MASSIVE ARMY TRUCKS WERE COMING UP FAST behind us on the highway, a row of them that was easily three deep. No flashing lights, but they didn't need them, not with the rumble of a half-dozen engines and the sheer size of them as they motored along.

"Fuck, what do we do?" Cowboy's hands gripped at Diego.

I put a hand over his. "First of all, point Diego the other way. If you squeeze the trigger, he'll have no choice but to shoot me, and at this close range, he won't miss."

The tension didn't leave him, but he did as I said and turned the big gun around. "Sorry."

"We're going to pull over," I said. "They aren't looking for us."

"Are you crazy? Of course they're looking for us!"

I shot him a look that had made men twice his size wet their pants and pulled over to the side of the road. The six army trucks shot by with barely a look at us.

For just a moment, I felt the brush of Eligor against my mind, but it was there and gone in a flash. Even so, the sweat started to roll down my spine. He could turn those trucks around and we'd be right back in deep shit.

But there was no slamming of brakes, no blowing of horns. They were after Peter and Carlos, just like we'd planned. "I hope Peter didn't pull over for a piss," I said.

We followed the trucks for a couple hours, and in all that time, Cowboy barely moved a muscle, fear radiating off him. I flicked on the radio, skimming through the channels for a news station. I finally found one, but there was nothing I needed from it. Just the weather, the upcoming events for the weekend, and how the local baseball team was doing in their first games. I left it on in the hope that something useful would come through.

"They were on their honeymoon," I said. "That's how I knew."

Cowboy shot a look at me. "What?"

"The house. There was a sign stabbed into the lawn that said, 'Honeymoon Happiness.' So there was a high chance they were on their honeymoon. Most couples have two cars, so I figured they would have driven one to the airport and left the other behind."

He twisted in his seat. "What are the chances of finding that, though? I mean when you need a vehicle?"

I shrugged. "Not always a honeymoon, but in a suburb like that, there's always someone who's away. Different reasons, you just have to look for them. Vacations and death are the two most popular to leave a house empty for an extended period of time."

The trucks took the next exit that would circle them around to the west, which meant Peter and Carlos were doing what I'd told them to. I frowned. "They found the car very fast. Too fast. Even knowing exactly what they were looking for, there have been no drones, no helicopters. Which means they were already looking for us on the road."

Cowboy nodded. "Can Carlos hide them if they get too close?"

I squeezed the steering wheel. "Yes, but they'll know what both of his vehicles look like." Fuck. They might already be on Anita too.

My guts twisted. She was my ace in this plan, the one reason I could look away from Bear and face these fallen bastards.

The kid gave a low whistle. "Shoot, it's not like this in Texas. Not at all."

"Everyone gets along?" I couldn't help the laugh that escaped me. "I have to call bullshit."

He snorted. "Of course not, but it's not so outright, you know? It's more . . ."

"Human," I said. "Not so vicious."

"Yeah," he said. "I guess so. We fight about stuff, but we wouldn't throw each other under the bus."

That did draw a laugh from me. "Yeah, and how do you think you got caught this far into the purge?"

"I had been out in the mountains for most of the spring and winter, staying on the range like I said," he said thoughtfully, "working the cattle, keeping them safe from wolves. I can do it without shooting anything so everyone is happy." He looked at his lap. "I came back into town, went to my cousin's place where I stay in between cattle drives, showered, went out for drinks, then came back home and fell asleep. That's been my routine since this all started."

"With your clothes on?" I gave a pointed look at his torn-up jeans on the floor at his feet and the cowboy boots that had earned him his nickname. He grinned.

"I might have had a bit too much to drink. But those people are my friends. They wouldn't have turned me over. They knew I was keeping a low profile."

He was so naïve, it hurt my brain just to try to explain it to him. "Yeah, and how many abnormals did you see in the bar that night?"

"Just the bartender. Jax. He had a new truck he was telling me about, all decked out with extras." He sucked in a sharp breath and I gave him a tight smile.

"What do you want to bet he's being paid to alert them—the ones who took you and me—to abnormals? Just like Peter was," I said. "They'll use him, and he'll think he's safe, and then . . ."

"They'll take him when they think they've got us all," Cowboy finished for me. "Shit. I never would have thought it of him."

"Greed and fear make people do stupid things. They make them agree to do things that normally they would never even consider."

On my shoulder, Ruby gave a low sigh and a soft snort right into my ear. I reached up and touched her head. "The good thing is, they drove right by us. Which means the trackers in our bodies aren't working and there is nothing in the bags that could trace to us."

I found my hand drifting to the tablet I'd stuffed under my shirt. Maybe that wasn't entirely true, but until I turned the thing on, we were safe.

Opening the tablet would prove tricky. But I knew someone who might be able to help us.

Assuming he wasn't already missing.

Eligor sat quietly in the back of the sixth army vehicle as they shot down the highway, following the direction of the handler who'd connected as best she could with the Magelore. It wasn't much, but she kept them apprised of where he was at the least.

"We'll be on top of them in two hours at this pace," the driver of the truck said. Across from him sat Easter. Her heels drummed into the floorboard, a nervous tic Eligor had seen more than once with Susan.

"Excellent. I'd like to have this wrapped up by the end of the day," she said, only it wasn't Easter. It was Susan, irritated that she was having to do this at all.

As they raced down the highway, he closed his eyes and tried to breathe normally. He couldn't let her see he knew something she didn't. That one glimpse of Phoenix had proven to him that they were still tied. But he'd cut her off, or he thought he had. What he thought it meant was that she'd somehow tied herself to him on her own, something he would have thought impossible. He wasn't sure whether she'd meant to do it, although he didn't know why she would want to still be linked to him.

Then they drove right by Phoenix, although he shut down that thought as quickly as it came. Just in case someone was watching him.

It boggled his mind why he'd want to protect her, but she'd tried to save him. And she'd nurtured the greenhorns at the facility. She cared about helping others more than she would've liked.

"She killed a demon, once." Easter turned in her seat and looked him straight in the eye.

As if she knew what he was thinking. Or who he was thinking about.

"Who is that?" He pushed his glasses up, feeling the sweat gather along the bridge of his nose.

She smiled. "Your girl, Phoenix. She's a powerhouse. It'll be a coup for me to take her down. Mad props for me across the board."

He swallowed hard. "I imagine. I've seen her charts."

"Her charts probably only got half of it." Easter laughed. "But if you want, I can tell you how she faced down the desert demon, or how she killed the most powerful Magelore the abnormal world has ever seen, or how she shut down the myst that nearly wiped out the population."

He just nodded, not trusting himself to speak, and Easter proceeded to tell him about Phoenix's life. How she'd been tortured and trained, how she'd been molded into an assassin. She'd tried to run from it, not once, but twice, and both times her new life had been stolen from her. He bowed his head as she spoke.

"Are you *crying*? This is not a *crying* story." Easter laughed at him, and he kept his eyes down. He *was* crying. So much pain in one life, so much loss, betrayal, and heartache. So much death. It was no wonder Phoenix was as dark as she was and yet he could not deny that her soul was brighter than any soul that would be lost.

Easter kept on talking, kept on whispering about the things Phoenix had survived. The flames of Hell had tried to consume her, but she'd fought them for her son.

"Stop!" he yelled at last, putting his hands over his ears. "Enough. I can't hear these things. It's not possible for one person to have been through so much and still have a mind intact!" He struggled to swallow around the emotions that threatened to drown him.

"Why should I stop? You want to understand who she is, and why she does what she does, don't you?" Easter had gotten out of her seat and she jammed the tip of her previously broken wand into the soft underside of his chin, forcing his head up. "And in a few hours, you'll get to look her in the face and see her for what she truly is under all that. She's a killer, Eligor. A killer. And she fooled you. She'll kill you too, if you get in her way."

When he stared into her eyes, he saw Susan staring back. "I know that, Susan. You don't have to keep reminding me of my mistakes. I'm acutely aware of what I did wrong."

She jerked back as if he'd slapped her. "Why did you call me Susan?"

"That's the name of your handler," he said. "Just as I was Nix's handler." He used her nickname, feeling as if he'd earned it after being inside her head for a year.

Easter's face twisted, rage flickering in those gold eyes. "No one is in my head anymore, that was the deal."

"Of course, my mistake," he said softly. She stood and stalked back to her seat. He closed his eyes and tried not to think about Phoenix, or about the strange desire he had to leap off the truck and run straight to her.

16

THE SIGHT OF THE GLOWING NEW YORK SKYLINE DID something strange to my heart. This was where I'd grown up, where my family had been, and where most of my hunting of abnormals had happened. This was not home, but it was, in a weird way, my life.

Cowboy was asleep in the passenger seat as I navigated the still-busy streets of the Financial District, working my way in and out of traffic like a pro. I managed to find a place to park in Chinatown, which was close enough to my end destination.

Part of me wanted to walk the streets I knew.

I wondered if they would feel the same. The thing was, with my current blond hair, I doubted many would recognize me. "Cowboy, wake up." I shoved his shoulder and he startled awake, gripping at Diego.

"Easy," the gun grumbled. "I was sleeping too."

"They sleep?" Cowboy shook his head. "Really?"

"Yanking your chain, man." Diego laughed.

Reaching into one of the bags in the backseat, I pulled out a proper shoulder holster for Dinah. I slid it on, grabbed another handgun—non-speaking— and tucked it in the other side.

"Here." I handed Cowboy a handgun and a waist holster. He slid it on with minimal difficulty.

I rolled down the windows, then took Diego and strapped him onto my back. "Ruby, guard," I said as I stepped out of the car.

She gave a woof and put her head on the shoulder of my seat, watching. As people went by, she gave a growl that made them scurry on their way a little faster.

"We won't be long." I slid out of the seat, grabbed a button-down shirt from our stash and threw it on to cover the weapons, then started down the street that would lead us to the church I wanted. Cowboy strode along next to me, the heels of his boots hitting the ground with a steady cadence.

"So . . . is this like a haunted church or something?"

"Yes and no. It's got a resident demon, but he's not strong enough to cause us any damage, so he's been left where he is, mostly undisturbed and unknown." My jaw ticked. "He's kind of an ass—he has little man syndrome which makes it difficult to deal with him."

Dinah shivered in her holster. "Because a difficult demon is a rare thing?"

I slapped a hand over her, and she muffled an ouch, which was ridiculous, but Cowboy's eyes went wide. "She can't feel it, Cowboy."

"Oh."

Dinah laughed. "Let me have my fun. He's so green, he glows neon with it."

"I didn't tell you to stop," I said as we made our way up the street, crossed under an overpass and continued on. I could see the spires of the church up ahead, and already the air tightened around me.

Most people didn't realize that it was possible for a demon to live within the sanctified walls of a church. Then again, look at the fallen angels—they were hardly on the good side of the scale, yet most people would think them preferable to demons.

I was not most people.

The wrought-iron fence surrounded the cemetery, and I ran my fingers along the rails as if they were a poorly made harp, the sound strumming through the air.

"Waking the dead?" Cowboy asked, and I nodded.

"In a matter of speaking. I don't like sneaking up on this particular demon," I said.

"To be fair," Dinah drawled, "we haven't talked to him since you were still in your father's employ. You think he'll be mad that you've stayed away?"

That depended on what mood he was in, but I didn't see any point in saying so. The last time I'd spoken to him, I was hunting for an abnormal with an affinity for the dead. My hunt had led me to the church we were approaching and the demon—who at the time I'd thought was a new-to-me abnormal—had given me a tip, though I suspected he'd done it unintentionally. I hadn't been back since. Not since I realized exactly what he was.

We stopped in front of the church, the tall wooden doors closed and locked tight for the night. I stepped up and knocked hard three times, paused, and knocked three more times, then a third round.

"Three?" Cowboy asked.

"Witching hour," I said.

"Three, three, three," Dinah sang. "Six, six, six. All the numbers mean something. How can you not know that?"

Cowboy stiffened as the door unlocked and slowly slid inward. I stepped over the threshold and was hit with a blast of cold air that had nothing to do with any heating or cooling system. I blew out a slow breath and watched the air mist up around my face.

"Ornias," I called out the demon's name, "we need to have a chat, you and I."

An impossible wind snapped through the church and slammed the door behind us, the lock settling into place with a loud click. Cowboy jumped, but otherwise was quiet.

I headed toward the main part of the church, moving easily in the dark. The lights of the city streamed through the colored glass windows, and while it didn't exactly illuminate the place, there was enough light to navigate. I headed straight toward the front of the church where the cross was set up high behind the pulpit, and then turned my back to it. Cowboy had all but glued himself to my side as if he were taking Ruby's place.

"Ornias," I said his name again. "Stop fucking around. You have a problem that I think you're going to want to hear about."

The pews ahead of us flickered, faces fading in and out as that unnatural wind raced around and around the room.

Cowboy's swallow was audible. "Are those ghosts?"

No point in trying to explain how the souls had come to be here, or that they were feeding the demon.

"Yes."

"Mary mother of God," he whispered, and I winced.

Ornias roared an answer to Cowboy that filled the air in an echoing blast. "NOT IN MY HOUSE!"

I tucked Cowboy behind me, just a half-step. "Not another word."

From the back wall of the church, right where we'd walked through the doorway, a thick shadow detached itself from the wall. A long cylinder that moved like sludge, slow and unstoppable, it lacked anything approaching a human shape. As it passed the ghosts sitting in the pews, it touched each of their heads, sucking down some of their energy.

The shadow sludge stopped at the front pew and circled upward, still not forming into anything recognizable. Behind me, Cowboy was shaking hard enough that he bumped me more than once.

"Ornias. Ornias the annoying, apparently. That's what the books said about you when I looked you up finally. You know, I had no idea you were a demon when I came here last." I smiled at the shadow that undulated in front of us. The ghosts behind us had all slumped in their pews as if they could barely remain upright.

"You insult me in my house." The demon's voice was a growl, a rolling thunder that rippled outward. It slid over my skin and brought with it fear. A demon gift.

"You have a problem, Ornias. And perhaps I can help you," I said.

Laughter flowed from him. "I have my pets, and new pets arrive every week in this devil-spawned city. I have no problem."

"Ah, but that's where you're wrong. I think your brothers are coming to pay you a visit." I was taking a gamble, but surely the hellish tableau from Carlos's front yard confirmed we were dealing with the fallen. And while the fallen were different from demons, they had to know one another.

The thick shadow slowed its movement. "I have no—"

"Those angels that have fallen, are they not related to you? Do they not become demons if they fall?"

The rumbling hiss that blasted out of him sent a literal icy wind around us, and Cowboy grabbed my hip with one hand. I didn't blame him. My first real encounter with a demon had about sent my mind into a spiral.

I held up a hand. "I want to make sure you are not with them," I said. "If you were, you and I would no longer be friends. You know, like I'm no longer *friends* with Bazixal."

Bazixal was the demon I'd killed to save my son. The cost had been high, but I'd done it.

The wind died down. A bell chimed somewhere

high in the church, but I knew for a fact that no one was manning the bells at this hour.

The thick shadow slowed further until it barely moved, just a twitch here and there. "You have become less afraid of the darkness, Phoenix. That is interesting to me."

When a demon knew your name, you *should* be afraid, but I felt nothing as I stood there, waiting him out. He might be a lesser demon, but he had knowledge that I needed. "You're finally catching on. I am not like the others who come to you," I said. "I need information, Ornias. Don't make me call on Bazixal. Neither of us want that." I curled up my lips like I'd smelled something rank. "Killing" the demon had sent him back to Hell, but there was no actual death for a demon, any more than there was death for a ghost.

"What do you need to know?"

"Tell me about the fallen angels. I studied demonology after my run-in with our mutual friend" —Dinah snorted and I put a hand to her, shushing her before I went on—"but I have a feeling I'm not going to find out how to kill them on the internet."

The demon let out a long laugh that echoed through the church, a cold snapping wind rising with it. "The fallen are not demons, not by our standards. Many of them chose to fall, others were cast out of what the humans would call heaven. And I have no idea how to kill them. That is . . . as the humans say . . . above my pay grade."

"What would they want with abnormals?" I adjusted my stance, crossing my arms. Cowboy's hand had not moved from my hip.

Ornias curled around himself like a languid snake, shadow looping in on itself. "Nothing."

I stared into the smoky darkness. "That's a lie. You forget I can hear them, even from a pro like you."

The darkness swirled harder. "How the fuck would I know? They don't talk to me!"

Cowboy's hand tightened until it was painful and I dared a look back at him. His eyes were closed and sweat slid down his face. Jesus, it wasn't *that* scary. I turned back to the demon. "You would know because I'm betting you keep tabs on what fallen angels you can. You don't like them, correct? They have more freedom than a weak demon like you. And I bet they could cast you out of your church. A church you can't leave without being cast back into Hell."

He lashed out at me, and the cold snapped across my face like a slap, leaving the left side of my face numb. "Bitch, you mock me in my own house! Bringing with you a half-spawn!"

I changed tactics, ignoring his cryptic shot at Cowboy. "How can they be killed?"

His movement slowed. "You truly wish to hunt the fallen?"

"Sure, let's say that I want to hunt them. They are coming for the abnormals, Ornias. Aren't the spirits of abnormals your favorite meals? The ones that last the longest?" I tipped my head at an older man in the middle of the church. He'd been a priest, judging by the way he was dressed, but the slightly gold aura around him indicated he was an abnormal.

Ornias sighed. "I don't know how to kill them. But they aren't all on the same side. Perhaps you need to find a fallen and have a conversation with them." He began to pull back, taking the shadows and the cold with him. I watched as he slid up the back wall and melted into the wood beams of the church.

"Where could I find a fallen that is . . . friendly?" I asked. Eligor would have been my first choice, but as long as he was stuck with Easter, that wasn't going to happen.

"Look to the heights," he said. "They think themselves still able to fly even without wings."

The demon's voice faded; minutes ticked by, and the natural creaks and groans of an old building settled around us once more. The cold wind was gone. "Let's go." I took a step and Cowboy stumbled after me, still not letting go.

Once we were outside, I knocked his hand free.

"First encounter with a demon, I take it?"

"No," he whispered. "I didn't want him to recognize me."

That stopped me in my tracks. "Say again?"

"My mother dabbled in the dark arts. She—" He shook his head and finally opened his eyes, and what I saw there would have set me back on my ass if I hadn't been already braced for something bad.

"You're part demon." So that was what Ornias had meant by the half-spawn comment.

He gave a slow nod. "That's the source of my power surges, the glow you saw back in the facility before they knocked me out." A slow breath slid out of him. "The demons are looking for me. Or at least my father is."

"And you just walked in there with me?" I couldn't keep the shock out of my voice, but I made my feet start moving again.

"I didn't think there would be an actual demon in there. My mother taught me that churches were safe places. I thought . . . you were wrong." He jogged to catch up to me. "Can I still come with you?"

"You're an idiot," Dinah said. "You thought she was bullshitting you? About a demon?"

I glanced at Cowboy. "Demons can be anywhere that they are called. Someone called this demon here at some point, for some reason." I wasn't going to explain to him more than that. As someone who carried demon blood in his veins he should in theory know more than I about his own kind.

Diego made a raspberry noise. "I can see you have no way with the ladies. Maybe I should give you lessons? I could do that. It might take me years to teach you, but I've always liked a challenge."

On the way back to the car, I thought about the next step. We needed to ditch the vehicle, find a place to crash, and then work out a strategy for finding a "friendly" fallen. Too bad I wanted nothing more than to lie down and sleep.

And maybe see my boy again, to assure myself he was okay. Tell him I was sending someone to help keep him safe while I dealt with the monsters.

Ruby's barks caught my attention from up ahead. My jaw ticked and I hurried my footsteps.

The car was out of sight around the corner, but I could tell Ruby was pissed. Her barks were interspersed with the deep growls of a dog who meant business and was done with the fucking warnings.

We circled the corner to see four young men around the car. Their tattoos were visible under the streetlight, their street colors clear.

"Hey, shoot the dog!" one of them said. "I want that shit in the car. Boss says—"

The young man caught sight of me as I yanked Dinah free. He drew his weapon too, but I squeezed off a round first. He died as he went down, and I shot three more times, clean shots before the others could even react.

I kept walking, unperturbed by the fact that Cowboy had stopped walking. Dinah sighed. "That was good. Those little fuckers were trouble."

I tucked her back into her holster on my left side, stepped over the bodies and got into the car. Cowboy stood on the sidewalk, frozen for a moment, then slowly made his way to the passenger side and got in.

Ruby gave him a woof and he reached back to touch her. "You just shot those kids. They were human," he said.

"Those kids were murderers," I said. "Those tats on their necks? They indicate how many people they've killed."

He swallowed audibly. "How did you know that from far away?"

"I just did." I wasn't about to explain to him that the bad ones were obvious to me most days, loud and clear. Sure, I'd been fooled here and there, but rotten humans were easy to pick out. They weren't as clever as they thought they were. My intuition became more powerful the longer I was away from the facility. In some ways, it felt stronger than it had been before all of this had gone down.

That was why I hadn't killed Eligor and had in fact tried to take him with us. Because, despite all of the brain-picking he'd done, he really wasn't one of the bad ones.

That made me smile as I backed out of our spot and drove away.

"Aren't you worried about getting caught?"

"No," I said.

"Why not?"

I fought not to roll my eyes, reminding myself that these were all the same questions I'd asked of my mentor once. Mind you, I'd been a hell of a lot younger. And far more eager to learn. I'd known even then that I wanted to survive, and that meant learning everything I could.

"Because the human police have files on many, many bad people. Those four will have records, known beefs with other gangs, and the police, for good or for bad, will turn their eyes the other way. They'll say it was a gang-related hit, that they are looking into it, and then the files will get buried. They have better things to do than look for the person who took out four known thugs, making their lives easier and the streets safer."

I took a turn and headed north into my old neighborhood, in the hopes that there would be a few of my old contacts left. Not all were abnormals, so there was a chance. My eyes drifted to the high-rises around us, then shifted toward the Empire State Building. That would be one of my next stops.

Look to the heights? I could do that.

"Dinah," I said, "you remember that friend of Barron's? The one he worked with from time to time?" Barron had been a part-time lover of mine when I was young and stupid. I'd thought he'd run away with me, help me start over. But, ultimately, he wasn't that interested in giving up the money he made working for the different mob bosses. In the end, it had killed him. Which was a shame on many levels, but especially because I needed to get in touch with his contact.

"What was his name?" Dinah mused. "Harold something, wasn't it?"

"Harden, not Harold." Though I suspected he'd changed his name to Harden to look tough in a world where being tough started with how people perceived you. On that note, I pulled into a twenty-four-hour pharmacy.

"What are you doing?" Cowboy leaned out of the car while I went into the store. I left Diego behind, but kept Dinah in her holster, still partially hidden by the long button-down shirt.

The clerk looked up, took note of the gun, and went back to reading his paper. "No money in the till."

I moved up and down the aisles and finally asked.

"Where's the hair dye?"

17

I DROVE THE CAR DOWN NEAR THE RIVER, PARKING IT under one of the bridges. I threw the keys into the water and left the doors open. A pair of homeless men eyed me up. "Great place to sleep if you ask me," I said. I pulled two of the bags out, and Cowboy took the other. Ruby hopped out and paced around, eyeing up the men. She lifted her lips over her teeth but didn't make a sound.

They waited until we were a good fifty feet away and then went for the car.

"They could tell someone we were here," Cowboy said.

"Doubt it. I just gave them a place they could sleep in relative safety for a few nights." I set out at a jog, despite the weight of the bags. The exertion felt good on my muscles and I relished in the way my breath shortened and my lungs burned.

I led him and Ruby back into the city. I suspected a few of my hideouts would still be safe. Or safe enough.

The first was my family residence in Queens—or I should say my mother's residence. It wasn't that big or fancy. Just an apartment in an okay part of town. It had been my mother's before she died, and she'd used it as a retreat when things got too tense between her and my father. Which had been often.

I hadn't been to it in years. Hadn't needed a refuge until now.

Daylight kissed the sky before we made it to the apartment building, sweaty and aching. Cowboy muttered something about his boots not being made for running. "We'll get better clothing today. After we sleep," I said.

I let myself into the building through the back door, not surprised the code hadn't changed in all these years. Up the back stairwell, up five flights, and then through the door that led to the fifth-floor apartment hallway. The last on the right was ours, a corner apartment. Better views of the city, plus an extra window to exit if need be.

I walked up to the door and put my ear to it. No noise.

"You sure it wouldn't have been sold?" Dinah

asked quietly.

"The lease was paid for twenty years, along with maintenance and cleaning," I said. "Still a few years left on that contract."

I punched in the numbers on the keypad and the door clicked open. I dropped the bags and motioned for Cowboy to be quiet as I slid through the door in a crouch. The keycode worked and the place was supposed to be maintained, yes, but both those things meant very little in our world.

The two-bedroom apartment was a good size for New York, close to eight hundred square feet. Huge, really. My walk-through showed me that no one had been there for years other than the cleaning crew, and they'd been doing a piss-poor job, at best. I swiped my hand through the dust and rubbed my fingers together.

Cowboy dragged in the three bags and Ruby trotted ahead of him and went straight to the couch where she plopped herself down. A poof of air sent dust particles up, which sent her into a bout of rapid sneezing.

"You think we'll be safe here?" Cowboy did a slow turn. The skyline had brightened and the room was already heating from all the windows. I went to the far right of the couch and pulled the cord that slid the blackout curtains shut, sending the room into instant twilight.

"Safe for now. Door on your right is your bedroom. It hooks to the bathroom so shower, shit, shave, whatever. I'll take the first watch."

I motioned for him to go, then waited for the door to close before I pulled up a chair and sat. Twenty-four hours ago, I'd woken in the facility with Eligor's fingers in my mind and no idea when I would have the chance to make a break for it. Now, I sat in my mother's old apartment in the city I'd left behind trying to figure out which step to take next.

I blew out a breath and laid Dinah and Diego on the table. From one of the bags, I pulled out a cloth and cleaning supplies, then began to meticulously pull both guns apart, cleaning and oiling their parts.

"Ohhhhh, she has magic hands," Diego purred. "Magic, I tell you. Do it again, harder this time." I was ramming the bristle brush down the barrel.

"Like it up the ass, do you?" I pulled the bristle brush out and laid it on the table, then checked the barrel to ensure there were no stray pieces.

"You know," Diego said, "we are magical in a sense, imbued with souls and created by spells that not just any savage could pull off. I can feel more than you realize."

I paused. "You telling me you don't want me to clean you?"

"Shut it!" Dinah snapped. "I like it."

"Yeah, I know you do." I put my hand on her. "I

missed you, Dinah. This last year . . . I wasn't sure I wasn't going to lose my fucking mind."

"You and me both, sister," she whispered.

Sister.

I swallowed hard, not wanting to think about that aspect of Dinah. Her soul belonged to my sister, and when she'd died, she'd been stuffed into the gun. To help me when the time came. Only I'd not known for years that she was someone I knew.

Someone I'd loved.

I let my hands do the work they knew so well as my mind wandered through what I knew for sure, what I suspected, and what I had to find out.

Abnormals were being hunted hard, so much so, the abnormal senators had been stripped of their office. We were being purged out of cities, and human law had been skewed against us.

Fallen angels seemed to be at the head of it.

I needed to find young Harden and get him to hack the tablet to see if we could find out why they were going after abnormals. Because it didn't feel like it was just as simple as knocking us out of the playing field.

And I needed to find a fallen angel so I could grill the shit out of him or her. The Empire State Building would be the best starting point for that plan. Old school in the clouds.

I must have been talking to myself under my

breath because Dinah spoke up as I finished putting her back together. "And where does Killian fit into all of this? You got Bear covered but what about hot stuff?"

"Who is that?" Diego asked.

"Killian is her man," Dinah said. "A hot-as-sin Irishman who quite frankly I'd like to see down his pants too."

"Ah, family. I get it. Save the family or stop the bad guys from doing terrible things that might get to your family." Diego gave a shimmy on the table. "Tough decision."

I leaned over the table and closed my eyes, struggling to breathe through the emotions. I'd faced this choice before, and it hadn't gotten any easier.

"Fuck," I muttered as I got up and went to the small pantry. There were preserved army food bags, and I ripped one open, added water and stirred it up. Once it was somewhat glutinous, I poured it into a bowl and tossed it into the microwave.

While it heated, I paced the small kitchen. Bear had said he was safe enough, but he looked like he'd been through shit. He'd been without me for another year of his young life, again believing I was dead. No, that wasn't true; he'd been told I was dead and this time he hadn't believed it at all.

"If you go to him now, they'll follow you right to

him," Dinah said, stopping me in my tracks. "You have to deal with this first."

"You sound like Eleanor," I said.

"Who's that?" Diego asked.

"My other gun," I said. "She died protecting me."

Diego was quiet, no doubt understanding exactly what I meant. Eleanor had been pointed at me, and the only way to save me was to misfire. Doing so had destroyed all her inner workings, killing her a second time.

The microwave dinged and I pulled out the now piping hot bowl and went back to the table. Dinah sighed as I sat next to her. "You know I'm right. If they are hunting abnormals, they'll want Bear. He's like you, strong."

She wasn't wrong. "I'm a shit mother," I said as I scooped what was likely supposed to be some sort of pasta dish into my mouth.

"No. You're a mother bear," Dinah said. "And mother bears are mean-ass motherfuckers who get shit done. You love your boy, and I love . . . you know, I love him too." Her voice caught, and I knew she was thinking of her own child. She'd had a daughter before her soul had been stuffed into a gun, and Emerald was out there too. Missing.

That was why Easter had Dinah when they'd been caught by the facility. I'd been pregnant, unable to go looking for Emerald and so I'd asked Easter. I knew that Dinah would do all she could to help Easter find her child. But it hadn't happened that way, not at all.

"We'll do this, then we'll find them both, Dinah. I swear on my life, I will do all I can to find her," I said, my voice low.

"Okay. Then let's kill these assholes that have put us into the position of walking away from family even if it's the right thing to do," Dinah said. "I've got your back, you know that."

I covered her with both hands. She was right. We had a job to do, and that job was going to get fucking ugly before it was done.

Scarfing down the rest of the meal, I made myself swallow the food even though it stuck in my throat. Next was the shower. The showers in the facility were lukewarm water, and you had only three minutes.

I got the box of hair dye from the bag and took it with me. They'd dyed my hair blond back there, part of their ritual of making me someone I wasn't. They'd done it to a few of the abnormals.

An hour and a half later, I stood in front of the mirror, looking back at a person I recognized. Jet-black hair, dark eyes, scars littering my collar bones and upper chest.

Scars of the past that had made me who I was. I

shook my head, dried off, and went out to the main living area, still wrapped in the towel.

The clothing I had was Rosita's, and while it was fine for a cut and run, we were in the middle of a fight that required a bit more than running shoes and jeans.

I dug around in the one bag. Peter had stripped several of the downed soldiers of their clothes, aiming for those that would be a closer fit to him and Cowboy.

Nothing in my size. I blew out a breath and looked down the hall. My mother's room was at the end. I made myself walk there, made myself open the door and step into her sanctuary.

The bed was a king-sized mattress in a four-poster Edwardian-style frame that dominated the space. Really, there wasn't room for much else. I sidled past the bed to the closet and pushed the doors open.

Inside was an array of clothing and a puff of stale air that smelled like my mom, of her favorite perfume. Honeysuckle and clean linen. I slowly pushed through it, looking for something that would work. My mother had been a pet, in essence, a kept woman who lived on the whims of my father. Which meant she had to dress the part.

The feel of leather stopped my hands and I pulled out the piece of clothing. Leather pants?

"Mom, look at you," I muttered as I untangled them from the hanger.

"What did you find?" Dinah yelled from the kitchen. I went back and scooped her up, paused, and scooped up Diego too. "Wait, why is he coming?"

I put the two guns on the bed next to the leather pants. "Oh, nice! Those are good quality too, no cheap-ass pleather!" Dinah chirped.

I kept on pushing through the clothes, feeling more than looking. My hands stalled on something hard, stiff. I tugged the article out and snorted at the boned bustier. I looked it over. "Dinah, I think this has a spell woven into the fabric."

"Shit, really? What was your mom up to?"

As if I needed another question with no answer. "No idea." I dropped the towel and snugged the bustier on while Diego let out a low whistle.

The arrangement of the straps allowed me to put it on without any assistance. As I finished setting up the last buckle on the front, I turned to the bed. "See anything different?"

"Nothing," Dinah said. "What do you think the spell is for?"

I ran my hands over it, thinking about why Mom would have needed spelled clothing. And why a corset? Of all the impractical pieces of women's clothing, this was one of the worst. Although, to be fair, this one had molded to me even with the boning in it. I scooped up a pair of undies and slid them on —imperative when wearing leather pants—and then pulled on the pants.

I stood and lifted a leg, settling into an old yoga pose, then slowly moved through a series of tai chi motions that tested the limit of the clothing's flexibility. Which was stunningly good.

"How do they feel?" Dinah asked.

"Magical," I muttered, barely holding back a smile. "Like they were made for me."

"Or your mom."

I nodded and dropped my hands to the floor in a forward bend. The clothing felt like something I'd wear to the gym to work out in.

"Your tits aren't falling out," Diego observed. "That is disappointing."

Dinah snort-laughed at him. "Like you'd even have a shot of being shoved under her shirt. You're too big."

"Yeah, baby, I am too big," he drawled.

They bickered back and forth about that while I searched the closet for more clothing. The basics were easy, but if there was more of this magic wear shit, I was taking it.

But there was nothing else even close to the magic corset, which was a bit of a downer. I pulled on socks and a pair of ankle boots made for walking. I tried a few more moves, all decked out, and was pleased with the results.

"Good thing your mom was the same build as you," Dinah observed.

I nodded, scooped up the clothes I'd pulled out, and went back to the living room. There was a mid-sized TV that I clicked on—not with the remote, the batteries were dead, but with the buttons on the side of the TV. I flipped through the channels until I found the one I was looking for.

Channel 9.75.

Yes, the abnormal world had taken to Harry Potter just like the rest of the population, and they liked to use it for their code words and entry points. Killian had told me about this one. Before I'd met him, I'd been considered human, a hunter of the abnormals, and they kept their secrets closer than a granny fighting over the last ball of yarn at a sale.

The channel flickered to life but with nothing but static snow. I left it on with the volume low as I went to work on sorting out the items from bags at my feet. Weapons and ammo into one pile, tactical gear in another, wallets in my lap.

I took the cash out first and set it aside. The credit cards were a no-no, of course, the perfect way to pin us down. I didn't look at the pictures of their families that they kept.

That was the way down a path of regret that didn't fly in my line of work.

"Hello."

The single word came from the TV and my hands stilled.

"Hello," the voice said again. "Raids on the east side of Queens."

The TV flicked off on its own. East side of Queens. That was where we were.

"Fuck."

I scooped up Dinah and Diego, putting Dinah into her holster and keeping Diego in my arms. The fallen cast sleep spells over the buildings they hit, that was what Peter had said. I crept to the curtains and peered out. It was closing in on noon. Would they really raid in the middle of the day?

The building directly across from ours lit up like a giant five-hundred-watt bulb had been turned on. I shaded my eyes but didn't look away.

"What's happening?" Cowboy stumbled into the room and peered out with me.

"Raid," I said.

"During the day? I never heard them raiding during the day, always at night."

"My thoughts exactly. Either they're on to us, or something has changed." I frowned.

The steady thump of helicopters slid through the walls and I peered into the sky. Three huge helicopters hovered above the building across the way. Something like fairy dust fell from them, all over the building. It sunk into the stone before ten seconds had passed.

Next came the army boys sliding down ropes, landing on the top of the building armed with . . . I yanked out a pair of binoculars from the bag and watched through them. "Tasers. Not guns. Why aren't they just killing them?"

"You say that as if it's better," Cowboy said. "You want them to die?"

"You want to live trapped like an animal? Forced to lose your mind?" I spoke absently as I watched the tactics of the trained men. Not that I thought they were all that good. On the contrary, they were sloppy as hell as they made their way into the building, not checking their points, not watching their backs.

I swept the binoculars up to the helicopters.

"No winged monsters," I said softly. I couldn't quite pinpoint why, but I had a notion that a ride-along was going to happen sooner rather than later.

"What are you thinking?" Cowboy asked. The look in my eyes must have clued him in, because he followed up with, "Oh, shit. Why?"

"Not today," I said.

Cowboy let out a sigh of relief. "Seriously, I thought you were going to jump through the window."

"It would have been the roof with a grappling hook," I said. "We're close enough."

He laughed but that laughter died out when I didn't laugh with him.

"You're crazy."

"Likely. But I know it."

The sloppy army joes were spilling back onto the roof, tugging along two people. I assumed they were abnormals. Limp, sleeping, unaware that they'd just been tagged and bagged.

I put the binoculars down. "Since you're up, keep watch." I flicked channel 9.75 back on and let the static flow.

Taking Dinah and Diego with me, I headed back to the far bedroom. "Three hours, don't let me sleep any longer than that."

I shut the door, laid the two guns on the bed and then lay down next to them.

"You got a plan?" Dinah asked.

I closed my eyes, tried not to think about my mom here, hiding from my asshole father. "Yes. We're going to find Harden first. Then we'll hunt us up a fallen angel."

"And kill things?" Diego asked, hope in his voice.

I breathed out slowly. "Yes. We're going to kill things."

18

I FOUND BEAR IN MY DREAMS BUT DIDN'T CALL HIM TO
me. He was sleeping too. Sleeping, which meant he
was hours ahead of us, still somewhere in Europe. I
bent and brushed a hand over his face, sweeping
back his dark hair. He was going to break hearts one
day with his striking features and fierce belief in
doing the right thing.

"You'll be better than me," I whispered. "I'm
going to shape this world so you can be better than
me. So that you don't have to be the monster I am."

I stepped back from him and let myself just sleep.
It seemed only minutes later that Cowboy was
shaking me awake. "Three hours and five minutes,"
he said.

I sat up and brushed my hands through my hair.
"Did you eat?"

"Yeah."

"Leave most of the stuff here. For now, it's home base." That being said, I had one other place we could go if we needed to. I wrote a note on a piece of paper and stuck it to the door.

"No cleaning?" Cowboy quirked an eyebrow up. "It could use a good cleaning."

"You want someone pointing out that there are bags full of weapons?"

When Ruby followed me out, I closed the door and started down the hall. I'd pulled a T-shirt on over the corset. Dinah rested in my shoulder holster along with a second gun. Diego was on my back, also under the very loose shirt. The T-shirt hid the guns and the tattoo on my back. The underbelly of New York knew me. I pulled an army green cap down on my now-dark head. Cowboy had on a pair of sunglasses and had changed out his boots for a pair of army hikers, and his flannel shirt for a white T-shirt.

He fit in better now. We both did.

I led the way out of the building, down to the street, and headed straight for the building across the way.

Cowboy grabbed at me. "What are you doing?"

I slid between traffic, Ruby next to me, flipped off a driver who honked at me, and was across the street in a matter of seconds. Cowboy worked hard to keep up, doing better than most trying to move through the traffic like a native New Yorker.

"I want to see if there's any residue of the spell." I worked my way around the building, careful not to touch the stone. Here and there, spots on the building continued to glitter from the spell that had rained down on the place.

I ran my fingers over the brick. Parts of it were warm, as if it had been in the sun, but this side of the building was in the shade. I looked up and down the alley, then stepped out. I snapped my fingers and Ruby came tight to my side.

"What do you think?" Cowboy asked.

"You touch it, see if it gives you anything." I pointed at the still-shimmering brick I'd put my fingers on.

He reached out and jerked back like he'd been bitten by a snake. "That fucking burns."

I put my hand back on the brick, once more feeling the heat but no burn. "Interesting."

Cowboy tucked his hands into his pockets. "Not really."

I reached out and took his arm, pulling out the hand that had touched the brick building. Heat blisters filling with pus, and worse, spread across his fingertips even as I looked at them. "Shit. We need to get you something for this."

I glanced at the building one last time as we left

the alley and headed down the street. I took us to the closest subway entrance, paid our fares, and slid into the first train that would take us back to the Financial District.

Cowboy clutched his hand at the wrist. I looked again. The welts were spreading from his fingertips across his palm, creeping toward his wrist.

Ruby gave a soft whimper and bumped her head against his thigh. Sweat ran down his face as he stood leaning against one of the poles. "I'm not much help to you, am I?"

"No," Dinah said and I shook my head.

"Not yet. But you don't throw away a tool just because there's not an immediate need for it. You wait until you can use it." I slipped an arm around his and dragged him off at the next stop. Heat radiated off his body and I knew we needed to get some hacka paste—and fast. The thick red goo had serious magical properties and could draw poisons out of your system as well as heal wounds.

The trick would be to find someone who had any left. With the abnormals gone . . . well, there was one place that had sold all sorts of goodies. I just had to see if the proprietor was still around.

Up the stairs and out of the subway we went, me on one side of Cowboy and Ruby on the other keeping him somewhat pinned between us.

When he stumbled and went to his knees, I knew

we weren't going to be able to make it on foot. I hailed a cab.

"Why aren't you yelling at me for fucking up?" Cowboy wheezed.

"I told you to touch it. I can hardly get mad at you for doing as you're told," I said as a cabbie screeched to the curb and I opened the door. I shoved Cowboy in, Ruby followed him, and I took the font seat.

"Corner of Third and Rochester," I said. "Yesterday."

The cabbie gave me a quick look, saw the butts of my guns and took off into the street, followed by a rather unharmonious blare of horns that was not unexpected.

"Your friend sick?" he asked, giving a quick look at the sweating, pale, pupil-dilated Cowboy in the backseat.

"Bit by something," I said. "Something he's allergic to."

"I have an EpiPen," the cabbie said.

I stopped him as he went for the dashboard. "Won't work, we need to get to our stop." I splayed out a few twenty-dollar bills from my small stash, three times the fare for the short distance.

The cabbie nodded. "You got it, darling."

I didn't correct him, though Dinah gave a snigger. I slapped my hand over her, then twisted around to look at Cowboy. "Hang on."

His jaw was locked and his eyes stared into mine as if he were seeing through me. "Trying."

Two minutes later, the cabbie pulled over. "Traffic is bad up ahead. It'll be faster to walk from here."

I didn't argue with him. I could see the myriad of orange construction signs and cones up ahead. I moved out of the cab quickly, opened the back door and dragged Cowboy out. Ruby leapt onto the street ahead of us and people moved out of her way.

With Cowboy's arm slung across my shoulders, I forced him into a stumbling, out-of-cadence jog. "We have to move."

"Trying." He bit the word out through clenched teeth.

We were a block away and I could see the old grocery store was no longer there. Someone else had taken over and created a souvenir shop. Fuck. Shit. Damn. I tightened my hold on him and kept on moving toward the space that had once been an entrance to a fixer-upper shop, if you will.

Our only hope for Cowboy was that there was still an underground below the new shop. We reached the big glass doors as a pair of oversized tourists in matching "I love NY" T-shirts tumbled out beside us. "Ruby, let's go." I nodded and she slipped through the open door without hesitation.

I was right behind her.

Humans scattered away from me and Cowboy as

I shoved my way past the stuffed plushies, mugs, T-shirts—wait. I paused in front of a stand that held lighters and snagged one.

"Hey, you have to pay for that!" a scrawny clerk yelled.

"Ruby, say hello," I said.

Ruby gave a snarling growl and stalked forward, her hackles rising and her chuffing woofs coming from deeper and deeper in her chest. If the people had scattered before, it was nothing to how fast they moved now. The shop emptied as people went streaming out behind us.

I all but carried Cowboy through to a small room at the rear of the store. I let him down as I went back to the door that we'd come through, shut it, and threw the lock. It would buy me some time to figure out what the fuck I was going to do.

No doubt the cops would be called. Cops who knew me if my shit luck was holding.

It couldn't be helped, not if Cowboy was going to survive. I hurried back to him. He groaned, but I didn't have time to comfort him. "Ruby, find . . ." I didn't know how to tell her to look for an abnormal. My old dog, Abe, could have done it, but only if I'd given him something to smell.

We were in a storage room, and there was no trap door, no door that led out except to the back alley of the building. I put my hands to my head, wracking my mind for how to find the hidden entrance.

"Fuck, I can't believe this." I dropped to the floor and took a deep breath, hoping . . . there! Just the faintest scent of abnormal. "Ruby, here." I pointed and she snuffled, and then she was off and following the scent to the back wall. I followed her, shoving boxes out of the way. There was no door. Her nose jammed against the connection between wall and floor.

I pulled a knife as Cowboy let out a low gurgle. "Fuck, hang on!"

I had to keep him alive.

He was too young to die like this.

I jammed my knife into the boards and pried until one board came loose. Underneath, there was a face peering back up at me. One I knew.

"Goddammit, don't be a cunt. I've got a dying man here!" I snapped.

"NIX?" The spluttering man spewed spit into my face. I stepped back as the floor beneath me dissolved and showed a set of steps. A tiny man wrapped in a long traditional Chinese kimono all but floated up the stairs and hovered over Cowboy, narrowing in on his hand. "Oh yes, very bad, very bad indeed. Let him die."

"No." I glared at him. "Fred, you help him!"

"He's part demon, let him die."

Sirens wailed, police sirens. I grabbed Cowboy and pulled him up and onto my shoulders in a dead-lift that even impressed me.

"Still so strong," Fred said.

I was already moving, passing the strange little man on my way to the stairs. He wasn't Chinese any more than I was, but he liked the style of clothing.

Ruby followed me and then Fred followed behind her. He sealed up the entryway as feet pounded above us. We were safe.

For now.

I stood in the semi-darkness, waiting for Fred to turn on a light. When it came, it was in the form of a candle. Not the safest considering the building timbers were still the original wood beams.

"This way," Fred waved for me to follow and I did. The space around us was too narrow and made me think of a mine shaft. "Here, here." He stopped in front of a too-small door and I had to put Cowboy down in order to get us both through. On the other side was a far larger room with two beds and a wall full of medicinal ingredients.

I laid Cowboy down and Fred went to work on him, slathering his hand with a thick red paste and lighting it on fire. The sparkles in the paste shot into the air and then ghosted down onto Cowboy's face, sinking into his skin.

"He's close to death," Fred said. "I don't know if

he'll pull through." He moved around Cowboy, touching various points on his body, shaking his head and clucking his tongue. His white hair was pulled back in a thin braid that ran all the way to the floor, and his almond-shaped eyes narrowed as he worked. Almond-shaped, but the deepest amber color I'd seen in a soul outside of the wolves in Montana.

"He'll either pull through by midnight or be dead. Nothing else I can do," Fred said.

I slumped and shook my head. "It was my fault."

"You make him a demon?"

I briefly told Fred about what we'd seen at the apartment building, how I'd touched the stones and asked him to do the same.

"You didn't know it would eat him from the inside out. Not many abnormals have true demon blood running through them, not even you, despite what you might think." Fred motioned for me to follow him, though that would imply we went to another room. No, he sat me down at a small table barely big enough for two and proceeded to make a pot of tea using a bare kettle and sprinkling some sweet-smelling herbs directly into the water. "How are you here? Last I heard, all the dangerous ones were taken."

I grimaced. "I could ask you how you were not taken."

"They don't look underground. Not yet. There are some still hiding deep in the subways, under buildings like me, and I have a few things up my sleeves yet." He sprinkled a few more packages into the teapot, then handed the empty papers to me to smell.

"I don't think you'd try to drug me," I said. "You liked Killian too much."

Fred smiled, but it was sad. "For a bad man, he was very good. Like you."

I shook my head. "I feel like I've woken up into a nightmare, Fred." I couldn't explain to him how good it felt to talk to someone who would understand. Cowboy was young; he hadn't seen enough of the world to realize how ugly it could be, and maybe now he never would.

"Yes, it is bad. But you are here now. Maybe there is hope." He poured me a cup of tea into a mug that read "I love NY." I couldn't help but notice how many of his mugs, tea towels, and general paraphernalia had that slogan emblazoned on them. I smiled as I took a sip. The warm tea was good, not overly sweet and just what I needed. No, I needed Fred and his amber eyes.

"Tell me what you know," I said.

"The purge"—he paused and took a sip before going on—"was just a cover. It wasn't even political, though it looked that way in the beginning. Most of the population didn't even care that we existed with them. They looked away, and we pretended we were human, and we paid our taxes and . . . that system worked."

I didn't nod, just watched him as he told his tale.

"There are multiple facilities, and some sort of abnormal seems to be running them. That is all I know, and even that is based on rumor and speculation as much as what I've seen with my own eyes. As soon as it got ugly, I burrowed in." He made a waving motion with one hand to encompass the space we were in.

"I think . . . it's a different kind of demon, a fallen angel on a crusade or some such shit, but I'm not sure yet." I took a sip of the tea, tasting cardamom and ginger, a hint of something else. Maybe pepper.

Fred's eyes widened, looking like glowing lanterns in the dim light. "Who would be fool enough to call a fallen angel to this side? To destroy us? Not a human!"

Part of his charm was his belief in the humans, as if they were innocent children and not capable of making the same mistakes as an abnormal.

"I don't think anyone called them out of the ether. I think they fell, Fred, they *fell* from grace." His jaw dropped and I gave a slow nod, then took another sip of my tea. "I have a tablet from the facility I was in. I need to crack it. Is Harden still around?"

Fred blew out a slow breath. "If he is, Rio would know."

How was I not surprised? I was being pushed toward Rio on all fronts, it seemed.

He looked down. "I tried to help at first, but it was chaos in the early months. So many of ours went missing and I didn't know . . . I just didn't know what to do."

I reached over and put a hand on his trembling fingers. "Fred, Killian told me once that he believes that people are put into play every second of the day. Even if we don't understand how the things we do will spool out or where the ripples will land. There's a pattern to it. Maybe you hid because I would need you now. Because I need Cowboy and you saved him. I don't know if Killian was right, but I also don't think he was wrong."

Fred gripped my fingers. "He chose well in you, Nix."

I smiled. "I miss him."

Those words fell from my lips, and then they trembled and I caught myself fighting tears. I *did* miss him. I missed him like I had cut off an arm and tossed it away. Only I hadn't been the one to toss it. Part of me knew he thought I was dead. He wouldn't have let them take me otherwise. The other part of me said to stop being stupid, that anyone capable of breaking trust.

"Do you . . ." I had to stop and catch myself. Ruby laid her head on my lap and I dropped a hand to her, needing her comfort. "Do you know what happened? How was he taken?"

Fred blew out a breath. "We all thought you were dead, you understand? He said you died delivering your girl, and he was taking the children to Ireland—"

I put up a hand to stop him, staring at him as if I were not sure I wasn't dreaming. "What did you say?"

He blinked a couple times. "Ah, well, that you died delivering—"

"No. You said . . . children. Plural." I couldn't breathe while he reached for me and took my hands in his.

"Your daughter . . . she survived, Nix. Killian took her and Bear and ran for Europe as the purge hit."

Hot and cold, I couldn't understand how I could be both at the same time, but the two sensations roared through me, his words burning into my mind.

My daughter had survived.

19

I CLUTCHED AT FRED'S FINGERS AS TIGHTLY AS I COULD without hurting him. "Say it again. Please."

He smiled at me, his face wrinkling. "Good news is worth hearing twice, I agree. Your daughter survived. Killian took her and Bear and fled to Europe. I don't even know her name. He kept it all as hushed as he could."

I couldn't move. I lowered my head to the table and let the tears flow. My baby . . . I hadn't been allowed to grieve her, so I had pushed all thoughts of her down deep, and now she was alive? She'd be a year old.

Maybe she'd be walking? Had she said her first word? "She won't know me," I whimpered. I fucking *whimpered* but I didn't care. Pain lanced through me. Bad enough that I'd been taken from Bear again, another year together swept away on the tides of fate. But he'd known I would come for him. He believed in me.

What did my girl have of me? Nothing, no memory, no connection.

Rage began to boil through my blood, tempering the grief, hardening it into a killing steel.

I slowly raised my head as the tears dried on my cheeks.

Fred gave me a tight smile. "*That* is the Phoenix we have all feared. You will destroy them now?"

"Every last one of those feathered motherfuckers." I stood and paced the room. "Is there another way out of here?"

Change of plans. I would go to the Empire State Building now.

He watched me. "There is. Are you going to Rio first? He's the only one left with connections."

I nodded. "Not first. But I'll go to him. Then I'll be back for Cowboy. Either to bury him or take him with me."

Fred sighed. "I wish you wouldn't leave me with an injured half-demon. They can be . . . difficult when they wake up in an unfamiliar place."

He went to his medicine cabinet and dug through it. "Here, take these with you. Rio asked for them, last I heard. You can be my delivery girl."

I arched my eyebrows at the three small stones. "What are they?"

He grinned. "Ah, I'll let you ask him. That would be worth seeing from a distance." He plucked a piece of paper from a drawer and scribbled down an address. "Here. He has an ability with the dead, so be careful. He is not strong like the others, but he has numbers now that he is the only one left."

"Is he a dick?"

Fred tipped his head and let out a breath. "Yes. And no. He will see reason, I think."

And if Rio didn't see reason, I would find someone who did. He would either play by my rules or he'd be ousted from the game.

"Well, you don't mean to stay, do you? Let me show you the back door. It goes into another souvenir shop, so mind your manners." Ruby gave a soft whine and I paused at the door. She sat.

"Good idea, you watch over Cowboy," I said and she gave a soft chuffing woof and shook her big head. "Stay."

She whined again, and I pointed. "Stay."

A low rumble slid from her and I snapped my fingers and pointed again, but all she did was step forward. So much for her obedience.

"Take the dog," Fred said. "She'll just get in my way."

I doubted it, but I wasn't going to argue. "Fine. Ruby," I barely said her name and she was glued to my side, her one good eye looking up at me. The scars on her face were etched in deep, but she hadn't given up.

And neither would I.

Learning about my daughter had made me more determined to end this thing. If I hadn't been all in before, I was a thousand percent done with these bastards now.

The stairs that led up and out of Fred's lair were nearly vertical. I climbed to the top, pushed open the hidden door, and looked back. Ruby sat at the bottom, took a beat, then shot up and past me and out the trap door. I climbed the rest of the way and stepped out into a storage room. Fred hadn't been kidding. There were souvenirs everywhere. The boxes were stacked high and close together and I had to worm my way through the maze to the back door.

I opened it and an alarm went off. I didn't hurry; the worst thing to do was move as if you had a reason to run. A snap of my fingers brought Ruby back to my side and we started down the back alley, avoiding the puddles of accumulated filth off the shops.

The address Fred had given me was in the warehouse district, near the docks. That would be easy enough to find. But I doubted there would be a welcome sign on the door.

Still, that wasn't my first stop.

Empire State Building first. I didn't know for sure that the old building would be a nesting ground. It wasn't the highest, but it was iconic and stately, and for lack of a better word, it *felt* like it would be the place a fallen angel would haunt.

It felt right, and that was enough for me.

I could have gotten on the subway or taken a cab, but I wanted to walk. The distance would take me thirty minutes at best, and I needed the movement more than anything else.

"So . . . you gonna talk to me?" Dinah asked.

"About what? How we're going to burn them to the ground and salt the ashes?"

She shook a little. "No, I figured that was a given. I was thinking more about the fact that your girl had survived. I didn't want to ask before, but I assumed the worst since you only spoke about Bear. By the way, I did know you were pregnant when you gave me to Easter. I could hear her heartbeat when you put me on your hip. Why didn't you just tell me?"

I crossed the road, dodging traffic, before I spoke again. "I didn't want you to worry. You deserved to find your daughter too, Bea."

"Don't call me that," she said, her voice softer than ever. Bianca had been her name before, when she'd been . . . alive? I wasn't even sure how to say it. Before her soul had been placed into the gun.

Diego cleared his throat. "So you two really were sisters?"

"Half," Dinah said. "Same asshole father."

I strode down the sidewalk, and the people who caught sight of my face under the brim of my cap scooted to put additional distance between us. A cop car rolled past me, the cop on my side gave me a quick eyeball and then looked away.

Twenty minutes passed and I was closing in on the building, making my plans as to just how I was going to do this thing. It all depended on whether or not the fallen was where I thought he would be.

"Diego, get ready with a sedative round," I said as I took one last corner and the iconic building came fully into view.

I didn't slow my steps as I went through the large double doors. I dutifully paid for my ticket, said that Ruby was a support dog which, while I got the side eye, they didn't argue overly much, and went to the elevator where I stood next to a group of tourists also waiting for their ride up into the clouds. Dinah snickered. "Goody two shoes."

The man closest to me turned and shot me a look and did a double take of Ruby standing quietly next to me. She showed him her teeth, just a quick flash of white not even followed up by a growl.

"I'm sorry, did you say something?" His accent was thick, German by the sound of it. I locked my eyes on his, pinning him with a stare that had him swallowing hard and scuttling backward, muttering under his breath.

When the doors to the elevator opened, I stepped in first, turned and faced the tourists. Ruby let out a low rumble. "Room for one."

The German man bobbed his head and put his hand on one of the women with him, holding her back. "Yes, I think that would be best."

I tipped my head ever so slightly to him as the doors closed. The music in the elevator was soft and meant to be soothing as the ornate box chugged its way to the top. Ruby lay at my feet and put her head on her paws, for all the world looking like she was going to take a nap.

"You really think you'll find one of the fallen here?" Diego asked. "I mean, how can you know?"

"Because," I said, not really wanting to give my secrets away to him.

"Oh, just tell him," Dinah said. "I want him to stay so I have someone to talk to."

She didn't wrap that up with "in case we get stuffed into a box again." Which was what I'd done with my guns when I'd left the life of an assassin so many years ago.

"That won't happen again, Dinah. I will never put my guns down," I said.

She shivered. "Good. Now, tell him how you

know the fallen will be here. He's too dumb to realize that you've done this a time or two."

I checked the elevator; we were about halfway up. "Where would you go if you were the fallen, cast out of heaven for some reason? When you hunt, you have to put yourself into the shoes of your prey. This is where I would go, if it were me," I said.

The elevator binged and the doors slid open. I stepped out and snapped my fingers so Ruby stuck close. Not that I was terribly worried. She didn't seem inclined to leave my side. I made my way past the tourist shop full of tchotchkes and T-shirts emblazoned with NY and Empire State Building. I moved to the outer balcony that was caged in to keep people from jumping off.

A blast of hot air slid around me as I left the cool interior of the building. I went to the edge of the balcony and wrapped my fingers around the metal grating as I stared out over the city I knew inside and out. I dropped my hand to the top of Ruby's head, centering myself.

Here, this had been my hunting grounds for so many years, and there were very few parts of it I hadn't been in, that I hadn't killed in.

I stilled my body and waited, breathing in the summer air that was a mixture of heat and smog. My mind wandered and I found myself sliding into the meditation that had allowed me to mentally escape the facility. No longer cutting myself off from my real self, the world beyond the one I could touch opened and I saw Bear. He stared at me, his face a little more healed, but his eyes wary.

"Look for Anita. I sent her," I said. "Be safe, keep your sister safe."

His eyes widened and he nodded and then was gone. Why the wide eyes though? Because I knew? Or had something more happened?

My hands began to cramp as I stood there and the time slid by. The day passed and the tourists began to thin as the closing hours approached. I made myself move, stepping away from the view and making my way around the circular balcony as the employees did a pass looking for stray tourists.

It was not difficult to avoid them seeing as they were too busy flirting with one another to notice they were being outpaced by me and Ruby, and they quickly went back inside, grabbing at each other as they went.

Idiots.

"What about the cameras?" Dinah asked, snapping me back to the moment.

I moved to stand right under a camera and settled my back against the stone wall, and the dog again lay at my feet, her one good eye closed, totally relaxed. "Happy?" I asked Dinah.

"Better. I mean, you're all about going undetected

and here you are right in front of the cameras like a diva," she bitched at me, and I smiled.

"Thanks. I was watching those two getting cozy. Love is a dangerous game, one that too many people lose at. It boggles the mind that anyone plays it anymore," I said, thinking about Killian. I'd taken a chance on love twice. Once with Bear's father, and he turned out to be the biggest liar of them all; I'd had to kill him to keep not only myself but our son safe. Killian had . . . he'd shown me what it was to have a real partner, one who stood by you. I touched my head, my memories of the night I'd given birth raw and unsteady. I wanted to believe that he had let me go because he'd thought me dead. And not because he'd made a deal that they'd take me and he'd be free. Even that I could be okay with if it was for my children.

My heart still clenched, though, and I hated the emotion. Emotions would get one killed faster than anything else and I drove them all down deep.

A boom of thunder in the distance turned my head. Storm clouds thick and gray rolled toward us with an unnatural speed, darkening the already dimming light of the evening.

"Here we go," I said.

I didn't move so much as a muscle twitch as the rolling clouds settled around the top of the building, slowed and then parted. A figure dropped out of the clouds and landed in a crouch at the corner across from me. I stared, trying to piece together what I was seeing.

She stood, but that wasn't quite right. Her back was stooped and her body was rail thin. Wings that looked tattered and bruised were tucked in tightly to her body and seemed too small to support her slight weight. Brilliantly white hair was pulled back from her face in a single braid that hung long over one shoulder with a few tendrils escaping their bonds. It was tied off with a series of daisies that had wilted.

Bright blue eyes peered at me. "You found me awfully quick."

I didn't move from my place. "Ornias gave me the clue."

She snorted and shuffled a few feet closer, a walking stick appearing out of nowhere. She gripped it hard and leaned heavily on it. "He was always a right bastard, that one. You know, I stuffed him in that church all those years ago. I found it amusing to throw it in their faces that a demon could survive in one of their sacred buildings." She pointed to the sky with her stick and there was a distinct twinkle in those blue eyes.

This was not what I'd expected. "The fallen are—"

She waved her stick at me. "I know. They are also right bastards and need to be stopped."

Dinah wiggled. "Is this for real?"

That was my question, but again, I stayed where I was. "Yes. They are hunting abnormals to extinction."

The fallen one looked at me. "Might as well be slaughtering their own children."

Her words sent a whispered chill through me and I tensed, which brought Ruby to her feet. "What?"

"You think that abnormals are just an aberrant mutation of the human genome? Please. They are a product of the fallen fucking about with humans. I mean that in the most literal of senses." She smiled, and her grin was one of unrepentance and fuckery. I really didn't want to like her, yet her smile echoed something in me.

"I need to stop them," I said. "I need to find a way to stop Gardreel and whatever plan he's got going on." I used his name because he was the one I figured might be at the top of the food chain.

She tapped her walking stick on the stone, the way I would sometimes tap my finger while thinking. "Yes, I realize that. You will need a powerful weapon to stop him."

"She's got two," Diego said from my back, and the fallen smiled.

"Yes, special like those two you carry. You didn't think they came into your possession for no reason, did you? This moment, you standing between the world of the abnormals and the fallen has been predestined since your birth. You are the Phoenix, the one that burns, the one that rises on wings of fire." Her smile widened and her blue eyes locked on my own. "I should know. I helped name you."

Sweat broke out along the back of my neck and trickled down my spine as the clouds above us rumbled and rain began to fall. "What do you mean?" I asked even though I was beginning to understand where the pieces slid together.

Her smile widened.

Her blue eyes twinkled. "I was a badass too, so I suppose you come by it honestly." The pause between her words was long enough that I wasn't sure I wasn't hearing things.

"Granddaughter."

20

THE FALLEN STOOD ACROSS FROM ME, BENT AND FRAIL at the top of the Empire State Building with only a narrow walking stick to hold her up. And yet I was the one who wobbled and went to my knees. Granddaughter. Was she shitting me?

"You are . . ."

"The grand dame of you, the one whom all your abilities stem from and from whence you find your shitty attitude and ability to kill without truly feeling the deaths." She laughed after she said that, flashing her teeth again.

"How do you not look like the other fallen? You know, the ones with the leathery wings and extra arms?" Dinah asked. It was a good question. Seeing as my head was struggling to wrap around the current information.

"I am fallen because I fell in love with the man I was hunting instead of killing him as was my job. We had a daughter, and she was an abnormal, a lovely girl who had terrible taste in men. And, of course, she passed her abilities on to you. This is the way of our line. I was . . . a killer always, though it was couched in terms of justice." She waved her stick at the sky as if flipping it off. "Because of my service, I was allowed to remain here for the typical lifespan of a human, and I am very mortal and dying. That is my punishment. Better than being stuck with those self-righteous bastards." Another flip of her stick to the sky.

Dinah spluttered, and Diego mumbled something in Spanish that might have been *what the actual fuck is happening.*

I stayed on my knees a moment longer before pushing back to my feet, using Ruby to steady me. I took note that she hadn't growled at the fallen one once. "So I have the blood of the fallen in me?"

She nodded. "All abnormals have the blood of the fallen in them, granddaughter. All of them. No doubt it is why Gardreel wants to wipe you all out. Because you are proof of their sins that have helped to confine them to this world." She shrugged as if it didn't bother her one bit that she was one of those sinners. "That would be my guess if I were a guessing sort of woman."

"I need to kill him," I said.

"That you do." She smiled and her blue eyes burned with a fire I understood completely. "But only another fallen can kill their own."

The image of the fallen being turned from monster into beauty before he was sucked down into what could only be Hell rolled through my mind. "Not true."

She waved a hand at me. "It was the power of a fallen you used on another fallen. They won't make that mistake again. And you're welcome for that." She grinned at me and wiggled her fingers. The back of my skull twitched and it was though she were touching inside my brain. "They didn't even notice me there in the clouds, undoing the bonds that Eligor put on your mind. Filthy, all that." She spit to one side as if to make her point. "Filthy. They have no right to bind those that are our children."

I drew in a slow breath, pushing down all the shock in me. The focus was on the task at hand. "How the hell am I going to convince another fallen to fight Gardreel? That is what you're telling me, isn't it?"

"How in the *hell* indeed?" she murmured and tapped her stick on the stone. "I am unable to tell you outright. That is against some stupid rule that a rather pretentious featherbrain came up with." Another swing of her walking stick upward as she jabbed it toward the sky. "But what I can tell you is that *you* have faced the fallen before, only he went by a different name. You know there is nothing so terrible as a convert, either to the light, or to the dark." Her eyes narrowed and I found myself mimicking her.

I'd fought the fallen before?

My heart clenched as I understood at least part of what she was telling me. "Bazixal."

The demon I'd sent back to Hell; could that be who she meant?

The air around us crackled with rising electricity and the hair along my arms stood.

My grandmother—Jesus Christ, I couldn't even think it without my jaw wanting to drop—looked upward. "We are about to get company. I do believe the fallen have realized I am here, talking to you. Forbidden and all that nonsense, though it matters not to me, my life is near its end." Another wave of her stick and the sky above us opened as though she were parting the clouds.

Drenched in a matter of seconds, I stared at her through the rain, watching her as she turned to face three of the fallen on her own.

Before I could ask, she pointed her stick at the door that led into the Empire State Building. "Off you go, find your team, stop the fallen, and get those babies back."

I didn't hesitate, though part of me wanted to see my grandmother kick ass. I picked up speed as I made my way through the upper souvenir shop to the stairs. No way was I taking the elevator and getting trapped in a steel box headed south.

A push of my hip against the bar of the stairwell door and I looked back in time to see two of the fallen being held at bay.

The third, well, he was creeping through the souvenir shop on his hands and feet, hunched like an oversized dog. Ruby let out a low growl, her back tensed, and the fur along her spine stood up. I touched her collar and brought her with me. "We can't kill him, which means we need to outrun him."

"What about the sedative?" Diego offered. "Please let me shoot him."

I pulled my T-shirt off and brought the AK-47 around, pointing him at the fallen one. I barely sighted down the barrel before I squeezed off two rounds, both hitting the monstrosity clean in the upper chest.

He roared and stood, wings spread wide for a half a beat. The sedative darts dangled from his flesh and then he wobbled and crashed sideways into a stack of snow globes that shattered.

I turned and bolted down the stairs, Ruby's nails clicking on the cement stairs. Eighty-six flights ahead of us. I pushed hard, grabbing the railings as I went even knowing that I was leaving behind fingerprints. It would give the NYPD a thrill if they dusted.

We reached the bottom in under ten minutes but, of course, the main door was locked. I yanked Dinah out and blew a hole in the doorknob. Alarms blasted through the air as I pushed the door with a hip and slid out onto the street.

The city was never really quiet, so I got a few looks as I walked away from the famous building, a gun on my back and one in my hand, wearing a corset and leather pants. I didn't care. The first good alley we came to I ducked down, heading off toward the abandoned rail station.

That was as good a place as any to start, a known messaging site for a lot of the underbelly.

Using back alleys and dodging sirens, I made my way down to the subway and hopped a ride that would take us to the Lower East Side.

I could have leaned back in the seat as we chugged along, closed my eyes for a few minutes and snagged some rest, but I couldn't close my eyes and not see . . . my grandmother.

Dinah squirmed. "I can feel you thinking."

There was no one close enough to us to hear our discussion. "This is fucking messed up."

"Yes and no," Dinah said. "Like, are you surprised that you're being called on? I'm not."

Ruby placed her chin on my knee, and I put my

hand on the top of her head. My grandmother thought I was the one to stop the fallen, and in part, she wasn't wrong. There was really no one else strong enough left.

But finding a fallen to kill another fallen . . . the only possibility I kept circling back to was that she had put emphasis on the word *hell*. She had to mean that I needed a demon to help me. Why though? Why a demon? Circling, circling, I knew I was getting closer to the answer, I just had to find it.

Maybe the tablet would give me the answers I needed. Maybe Rio would have someone like Harden who could hack the tablet and find the answers we needed. That I needed.

"Wonder if Cowboy is okay," Diego mused.

I blinked. "It never even crossed my mind."

The subway car began to slow and I stood, bracing my legs as I scanned the car.

"This our stop?" Dinah asked.

"No, it's not," I murmured. "We're stopped in the middle of the tracks."

Which to me could mean only one thing.

We'd been found.

21

I HURRIED TO THE FAR END OF THE SUBWAY CAR AND GOT my hands on the doors. They were locked tight, which was not in my favor.

I pushed on them and was about to pull Dinah when the door at the other end slid open. I turned and dropped to a crouch as I raised Dinah and held her steady. Two figures stepped into the subway car and the first gave me pause.

Tall, blondish, super nerdy with glasses and bright blue eyes that were full of fear. He quickly ushered the few humans out of the subway car with a soft voice and a quiet demeanor.

"Eligor." I stayed where I was. "That was quick."

"Your discussion with Namaa alerted us," he said as he stepped farther into the car and was quickly followed by Easter, which was where my attention stayed.

Namaa. That must be my grandmother's name. Grandmother. Damn, I still couldn't believe it.

Easter's head had been shaved on one side and the remainder of the long strands of rich red were swept all to the other side in a low ponytail. She wore street clothes, but it was the wand in her hand that kept my eyes on her. She was a cleaner, the kind of abnormal who could make it look like nothing had ever happened in a crime scene. But that was not where her abilities stopped.

"I don't want to shoot her," Dinah whispered.

"No choice," I said. "We used all the sedative rounds on the fallen."

Diego gave a grunt but was otherwise quiet, keeping my little lie between us. The subway train got moving again and the car we were in lurched a little. Eligor stumbled, but neither Easter nor I so much as flinched.

"It's about time we had this out, you and I," Easter said. "You should have fought at my side when I tried to break free of that fucking facility."

I smiled at her. "You should have listened to me and had patience."

She bared her teeth and snarled as she lifted her wand in a sharp twist of her wrist. I squeezed off a round at her hand, wanting only to disarm her.

The bullet missed as she dropped and spun away from it, knocking Eligor to the ground. He yelped and crawled to one side.

"Please don't do this! Phoenix, there are men waiting for you at the next train station!" Eligor yelled.

"Shut your traitor mouth!" Easter swung a fist toward him, sloppy and loose as though she had no idea how to fight. Which wasn't her at all.

With her no longer looking at me, I shot again, this time hitting the wand in the middle and shattering it.

It broke like glass, shards flying throughout the small car and a pulse of energy blowing out with it that sent me tumbling through the air. Ruby yelped and went end over end, her paws unable to get purchase until she slammed into the end of the car. I stood and tucked Dinah away.

"Try not to shoot me," I said as I walked toward Easter.

She stood straight and settled into a stance.

Her fist snapped out for my chin, then she feinted and drove her left fist into my side. I took a step back and let her come at me, keeping my fists up, blocking her here and there. Mostly just waiting.

Killing people was easy.

Not killing someone while still handing them their ass required patience.

Easter kept at me, a grimace on her face as she shot close and tried to drive a knee into my belly. I crossed my arms, blocked her leg and shoved her back. I suppose I could have just shot her with the sedative, but I needed to see how deep the real Easter was. Or if there was anything of my friend left.

"Easter, snap the fuck out of it." I blocked another flurry of blows, pushed her back again.

"Time, you don't have the time!" Eligor called.

I glanced to the side to see that we were indeed coming up on the next station. Figures in army black and holding a shit ton of weaponry were visible even in that glance.

Easter took my moment of inattention and came at me hard, tackling me to the ground, and I let her. She got her hands around my neck and started to squeeze. I grabbed her wrists with my hands and dug my nails in enough to force her to relax her hold on me. "Easter, you're being ruled by a master."

Her face twisted with rage and I dug deep into my own body, looking for the power that made me what I was. That power that was an ascendant. My bloodline was from the fallen, so who said I couldn't do exactly to Easter what the others had done to her?

I closed my eyes and let myself fall into that state of meditation that had saved me. My hands went limp on Easter's and her fingers tightened around my neck.

Everything around me was distant. The sound of the car doors opening. The screaming of Easter as she strangled me. Ruby snarling from behind us, snapping her teeth at Easter. Dinah yelling at me to do something.

I blinked and stood in the fog of my mind and reached out with a hand to where I thought Easter should be, my fingers brushing against something.

Metal, it was like she was wrapped in metal that I couldn't see. I wiped my hands over the metal and it cleared like glass. Easter pressed her hands on the glass as she stared up at me, her mouth working but no sound coming out.

Help me.

I spun on one foot and drove a roundhouse kick into the glass and metal cage that held Easter tightly. I bounced off the cage and hit the ground hard, gasped and felt my heart stutter.

I was dying.

I needed to break this cage now.

A hand touched the back of my mind, Eligor making his presence known. "You have to use the power that is in you to break it," he said and then he was gone.

The power in me. That rage in me was red hot and it swelled up, a magic that was nothing but death and destruction. But even those things were good. They'd saved me more than once, and they were going to save Easter.

I placed my hands on the cage, and the power in me rolled upward through my fingertips and into the bonds holding her. A moment of pause, like the world held its breath and then the cage exploded around us, not unlike her wand. A scream of a woman who had to be the one controlling her echoed through the space, a screech cut off mid-scream.

I was thrown back into my body as her fingers loosened and her forehead dropped to mine. Easter's hair flowed over our faces, as close as lovers. "Took you long enough," she whispered.

"Impatient," I whispered back.

She grinned and pulled me to my feet. I stayed limp, falling into the roll that would save us both. Ruby whimpered, and I motioned to her with the slightest flick of my fingers. She settled and limped to stand where she could butt her head up under my loose fingers.

"I got her, boys." Easter lifted me into a fireman's carry over her shoulder.

We had it all going smoothly. I already knew exactly what she'd do. She'd take me out of the subway and we'd take whatever car was waiting for us and lose the army blokes. We'd get the fuck out of here, both of us free.

But neither of us had counted on Eligor not understanding that she wasn't hurting me.

Nor did I think he had it in him to try to stop her.

"No!"

Eligor hit us from behind, throwing Easter to her knees, and I fell from her shoulder, hit the ground, rolled and came up with Diego. Spinning to the army boys, I squeezed the trigger, spraying them with a barrage that sent half of them to the ground, and the other half running for cover.

"What the fuck?" Easter tucked in behind one of the seats as the doors to the subway car tried to close, getting stuck on the leg of one of the men I'd killed. She grabbed the downed body and pulled him so the doors shut. I ducked down and looked back at a still standing and very stunned Eligor.

"I thought . . . she was going to hurt you," he whispered.

"Get down," I snapped and he dropped to his butt as if he were Ruby, trained to commands that I could give in my sleep.

Easter snorted as she went through the dead man's gear, pulling out two guns and his flak jacket which she slipped on. "What are we doing?"

I noted she was ignoring Eligor. For the moment.

He, on the other hand, was staring hard at her. "You can't trust her. Susan is a terrible handler and

she hurt your friend to make her be able to kill you,"
he said.

I peeked up over the edge of the window as we
pulled out of the station, ignoring him. The army
boys were climbing into the cars behind us. "We've
got company pulling in."

"Why aren't you listening to me?" Eligor whispered. "Please, I am trying to help you!"

I grabbed his arm and pulled him to his feet,
pulling him behind me as Easter stood and started
for the door that would lead us to the car ahead.

"Here's the deal," I said. Easter shot the door
handle, flipped it open and did the same for the next
car. We stepped across the open space and I all but
dragged Eligor across with me. His face was pale,
and his skin slicked with sweat. I tightened my hand
on his arm and pulled him close to my face. "I
burned Susan out of her. Do you understand?"

His jaw dropped. "You . . ."

"I met my grandmother." I grinned as I said those
four words. I couldn't help it, and it was not a happy,
yay for a family reunion grin. More like a *I know all
your secrets, little man* grin and *I'm going to use them to
destroy you.*

Eligor managed to get his jaw closed and he swallowed hard. "But your abilities, I locked them away. I
didn't think Namaa was that strong!"

Easter shook her head, red braid flipping back

and forth. "Not the time to discuss. They're coming in on both sides." She motioned with her gun to the car ahead of us now and the flickering lights that showed the figures creeping toward us, weapons raised.

I turned to see the first group behind us in the previous car too. "How big of a boom can you give me, Diego?" I pulled him around and let go of Eligor. The fallen stumbled to the middle of the car and sat in a seat, clinging to the seat handles.

"Well, what are you thinking?" Diego rumbled.

"You got anything that will blow the coupling between the cars?" I made my way to the front of our car. Better to let that one pull away from us.

"Grenade?" he offered.

"Switch it out," I said. Easter blew the door open with her gun, and I stepped up to the edge and looked down at the track moving beneath us. I lifted Diego and barely squeezed the trigger. The grenade shot out and I threw myself backward. Easter was already on the floor as I landed beside her and the front of the subway car rocked upward, the explosion shaking the whole system.

Ears ringing, I lifted my head to see that the section ahead of us was pulling away. One set of idiots down, on to the next.

Ruby let out a snarl and I turned in time to see her launch at one of our pursuers. She clamped onto his forearm and dragged him to the ground, snarling and wrenching him around. His screams only seemed to send her into a further frenzy.

He reached for his side arm and I rolled to my knees, pulled Dinah and shot him in the head. His friends started to push their way through. Not understanding that they were coming right into a trap.

"Killing them all? Pretty please?" Dinah said.

In answer, I lifted her and shot the next two in the head in quick succession. They kept coming, though, through the funnel we'd created, dying on top of each other, stacked up like firewood.

Beside me, Easter watched and waited while Dinah and I did the dirty work. Not that I minded.

In under a minute, the men that the facility had sent after us were dead, and our subway car had coasted to a stop.

I tucked Dinah back into her holster, stood, and snapped my fingers for Ruby. She pressed herself against my side and I rubbed her head. "Good girl."

She gave the slightest of wiggles, her whole body getting into it for just a second.

"Ready?" I looked at Easter and she nodded.

"Let's go."

I took a step and Eligor grabbed my hand. "They'll find you again. I . . . I didn't bring them here. I swear it."

I looked down at him, feeling him try to get into my head and quickly shut that down. I pulled my hand free. "I suggest you run, Eligor. Because Easter and I are about to go hunting."

His face, which was already pale, went ghostly white. "You can't kill the fallen."

Easter laughed. "You were in her head all that time . . . how the hell do you for one second believe she won't find a way? She freed me, and you think she won't find a way to fuck up those who captured us?"

Eligor looked to her and then back to me. "They'll kill me, but they'll take my mind first. They'll know everything about you." He closed his eyes, then opened them again. "You have to kill me."

I looked at Easter and she shrugged. "We could use him," she said. "He has information."

That had been my thought, but I didn't quite trust myself when it came to Eligor. I believed his intentions were good and that made me trust him when I wasn't sure I should.

"Why?" I asked again, knowing that I was using up precious time, but despite my penchant for killing first and asking questions later, sometimes I did it in the proper order.

"You have to kill me," he whispered again. "They will find you through me and they will kill all your friends, your son, anyone they find to hide their shame."

I stood next to him and really looked at him. "Why do you care so much, Eligor? When the others were taking us down, why did you not hurt me? You could have broken me, and we both know it."

He started to shake, and a tear slid from one closed tight eye. "You are not the only one motivated to do what you do for the love of a child you'd protect."

A rush of air slid out of me. The fallen who was my grandmother had said as much, that the other fallen were wiping out their own children. "Is your kid alive?"

"No," he whispered. "I . . . broke her mind myself and . . ." a sob rippled out of him and he covered his face with his hands.

I lifted Dinah and pressed her muzzle against his heart. "If I thought I could kill you on my own, I would. But we both know that isn't possible. Is it?"

His eyes opened and I motioned for him to back up. He looked down at his feet and I squeezed Dinah's trigger. She gave a surprised *Ooh!* as the bullet slammed into him and flipped him over the bodies of those who had died.

"I wasn't actually expecting that," she said. "I mean, I'm all for it. But you just—"

"He's like Justin," I said. "At least in a way.

They'll find him and make him respawn into another body, and another, and another. But he's right. He can't come with us."

"So why shoot him?" Easter asked.

"Because they will hurt him no matter what, but maybe a little less if they think I tried to kill him so easily," I said.

I hopped out of the car down to the tracks. "Watch that third rail."

The lights of the subway car quickly faded as I led us back to the previous stop.

Down there in the dark, the sounds of the city were muffled. The smell of the homeless who lived here was heavy.

Easter and I moved quickly, jogging through the darkness, moving in quiet tandem.

The smell of burnt wood tickled at my nose.

I slowed and frowned, picking up the sharper intense scent of an abnormal that I normally wouldn't have found except that I had smelled someone like him before.

Easter took a sniff. "You getting that too?"

"Here, it's coming from here." I held up a hand and found myself stopping beside a service door. I stepped up to it and touched the handle. The door swung open and I was through, following the smell of someone I knew all too well no matter how impossible it was. Because they were all dead. Weren't they? Another strong whiff of abnormal with the blend of burning wood and I knew without a doubt who we were tracking.

Someone from my family.

One of my siblings was here in the subway.

22

EASTER DIDN'T QUESTION MY CHOICE OF DIRECTION. "You know who it is?"

"I am hoping I'm wrong." I kept my voice low as did she. This was not the time to be shouting about our presence.

I made my way through the semi-darkness with only emergency lights flickering here and there, leading us forward in conjunction with the scent that shouldn't have existed. The fact that the light and the smell were together made my skin crawl on my back.

My siblings were all dead. All of them. So who the fuck was I smelling? Maybe a bastard child of Romano's? I supposed that was possible, but he kept close track of all his dalliances and any children produced from them. I couldn't believe that any would have slipped his leash.

I followed the smell of my sibling—whoever they were—letting it lead me through tunnels that otherwise would have been nearly impossible to navigate. Luck came with being an ascendant. Luck and coincidence to help survive what would kill most others.

Which was why it was so easy for me to follow my feet and the freakishly familiar smell and not lose my mind over the ease of it.

The only sounds were that of water dripping and the click of Ruby's claws on the concrete. Otherwise, we were quiet. Dinah included. The three of us knew that silence was a tool to be used liberally.

Impossible, that was what kept running through my head, and yet there it was, pulling me through the darkness.

The light disappeared and I held up my palm, calling up my fire to pool, red-gold and brilliant enough to give us an easy path. Easter gave a low grunt from behind me, the tension growing.

A few more turns and we were in front of a ladder rising high above our heads. I bent and scooped Ruby up, settling her on my shoulders, then started the climb. She didn't squirm, didn't so much as flinch as I went up. I was breathing hard by the top, and glad she was no bigger.

The end of the ladder had no covering. I popped through and Ruby scrambled off my shoulders.

"Took you long enough to find me."

The words were not fully out of the man's mouth before I had Dinah up and pointed in his direction, even though I was only half out of the tunnel, my feet still on the ladder.

Ruby rumbled a low growl and settled into a crouch beside me, but otherwise didn't move, her one good eye locked on the shadows to my right. The speaker stepped out of the darkness and held up his hand, brilliant blue and green flames lighting it.

"Holy shit, he's like Bear!" Dinah yelled as I finished climbing the last of the ladder and stood across from the abnormal who smelled like family and held flames like me.

The pieces came together quickly, memories from before the facility flashing like intense lights. "You are the third ascendant, the one Mancini couldn't find."

He dipped his head toward me. "I am."

I still didn't lower Dinah. I was no fool to think that just because he had the same power as me, the same blood, that he was safe and not there to kill me or trap me. The flames rolled around his wrist and up his arm, absorbing into his skin. "I wanted to meet you before you came to me. God only knows what my people would do if they knew exactly what I was capable of."

He smiled and I saw a flash of teeth. He was fair-haired, blue-eyed, and taller than most. A sweep up and down and I put him at six foot four. Lean like a swimmer and with just the skim of a beard that was shades darker than his hair, he would turn heads.

He reeked of abnormal, though if he was a true ascendant, he shouldn't have. He smiled, and in that smile, I knew he was not there to kill me. At least not yet. I found myself lowering a spluttering Dinah.

"What the fuck are you doing? He isn't that charming!"

I drew a slow breath and the smell of abnormal faded. "He has my mother's smile."

He grinned. "Very good."

"What is this, fucking family reunion week?" Dinah grumbled from her holster.

Diego grunted. "Disappointed again. I was just hoping to shoot a few more things."

The man in front of me spread his hands wide. "I have been trying to get your attention since you escaped the facility. I did try to break you out once, but they buried you deeper than any other abnormal. Both of you." He gave a nod to Easter as she moved to my left with her gun raised on the ascendant.

"Let me be clear," the man said, "I am very much related to you, Phoenix. Closer than you might expect. Your mother—excuse me—our mother, gave me up for adoption before Romano took her fully. Thank you, by the way, for killing him. It was on my to-do list."

I just stared at him. Seeing the similarities. The differences. "Goddamn it," I muttered. "How the fuck have you stayed hidden so long?"

"I played dumb, same as you." He sighed and ran a hand through his hair. "But I cannot play dumb now. There are far worse things than Romano and Mancini at our heels."

Dinah wiggled in her holster. "Seriously? You think she's just going to believe you because you're cute? She has a man, you know!"

I didn't roll my eyes, but I felt like it. Sometimes Dinah focused on the wrong aspect and this was one of those times. "He's my *brother*, Dinah. Which means he's half your brother. Full blooded to me. Yes? And I imagine a couple years older?"

He nodded. "Yes. After our mother got pregnant from Romano the first time, she hid long enough to have me and give me away. But she still checked in on me when she could, and she made sure I had ties to strong abnormals to train me and protect me." He shrugged. "You are looking for Rio, are you not?"

Easter grunted and I nodded. "He was supposed to be the last real powerhouse left."

He held out a hand. "Nice to meet you. My friends know me as Rio. Mario is my name, though."

Mario turned and beckoned for us to follow him. "This way. There are things we need to discuss."

"No shit," Easter muttered.

I let Easter lead this time, wanting a little space between me and this Mario who was most certainly my brother. How I wished Eleanor was still with me and I could give her shit for keeping this little gem of a secret.

Mario led the way through this level of the subway, up to street level via a series of stairs that switchbacked. I thought he'd be silent through the walk, but he picked up a running narrative.

"I have several Hiders working for me which is partly why I've been able to keep things quiet. All along, I thought I'd take down Romano and take over his territory. Set it up for a more stable place to live for abnormals, but you beat me to that punch." He walked to an alley that opened on the docks. Jesus, we'd come a lot farther than I'd realized.

He led us across an empty dock that should have been bustling with people, but if anything, it was eerily silent. Easter glanced at me, her brows drawn down. I didn't blame her, but I knew when to trust and when to run.

It was why I'd survived all these years. It was why I'd known when to break out of the facility, and it was why I knew in that moment, at least in the space of the next hour, we could trust Mario.

"Since the purge, I've been gathering as many abnormals as I can, keeping us all in one place. It sounds dangerous, but the Hiders I have can keep everyone safe. We go out only when we have to. But things are getting tight and we need to find a way to deal with these new monsters." He approached a large brick building. "This is the closest thing to a rebellion headquarters as you're going to find. I've managed to intercept a few deliveries to the different facilities, but it's been difficult. The winged monsters they keep on retainer don't react to any weapon we've come up with. They don't like my fire, but I've been careful with that because if I go down—"

"The last of the abnormal world will sink," Easter said. "You're the last ship standing. That's what you're saying."

He nodded and pushed the wide iron door open. He didn't motion for us to go first, just walked in and Easter followed.

I stood in the threshold of the building, my nose assaulted by the smell of unwashed bodies and abnormals.

My eyes adjusted quickly to the inside of the building and I stared at the number of people there.

Maybe fifty, not what I was expecting. Because I knew how many abnormals there were in New York. Thousands. Tens of thousands. And I was looking at fifty.

Which meant the facilities were only for the strongest of the abnormals and everyone else was just . . .

Peter and Carlos, stood drawing my eyes to them. Carlos gave me a head bob, but Peter hurried over to me. "You made it. I wasn't sure."

I raised an eyebrow at him. "The facility gave up on you, did they?"

He nodded. "One second they were gunning us down, the next they were pulling a U-turn and headed toward New York."

Carlos made his way to me. "Your son is with Anita. She let me know he is safe with her, as is your daughter and their current guardian, a young female abnormal who has survived on her own for some time."

Relief slid through me, but I kept it in check. It would only take me a moment tonight to slide into the mists to be sure Bear and his sister were indeed safe.

"They kill those they deem unworthy of their attention from what I can tell," Mario said with a sweep of his hand.

Which reminded me of Cowboy lying underground, fighting for his life.

"You know Fred? The one who thinks he's Chinese even though he's as white as your ass?"

Mario barely held back a smile. "I do."

"Well, he's currently under the tourist shop on the corner of Third and Rochester," I said. "And he has a friend of mine. Kid can blow an EMP pulse if he pulls through his injuries."

Mario looked at a young woman whose dark brown hair was cut short, shaved along the back. "Lanny, go get him. That could come in handy if we can keep him alive."

Lanny slid on a pair of shades and all but disappeared from sight. Camouflage abnormal. Like a Hider but even rarer.

"I hear you have something for Harden," Mario asked as he led us deeper into the building.

"I do. A tablet from the facility." I pulled the pocket-sized tablet out of my hip pouch and handed it to him. Inside, I could feel the three rocks that Fred had given me to pass on to Rio. I hesitated on them, feeling this wasn't the right time.

He took it and tossed it to another guy who leaned against the wall. He flicked a tongue out and caught a few flies. Mario gave him a nod. "Harden, meet my sister. Can you crack that? Get the files and don't get caught."

"Betcha sweet assssss." He drew out that last S on purpose. I didn't bother looking at him after that. Acting tough was a sure way to show me how weak you were.

There was a tingle along my spine and my grandmother's words came back to me.

Gather your team. This was the place to do it. I

looked at Mario, really looked at him. He was ascendant, like me. Like Bear. I had a Magelore, Hiders, and Easter. A kid with an EMP pulse up his sleeve and maybe a few other top-notch abnormals.

Gather my team, and then I would have to do the one thing I dreaded. I would have to call up Bazixal. I was going to invite that fucking demon to my party because he was the strongest one I knew, and because I knew he would want to negotiate with me if he could.

That demon had lost me once. He wouldn't want to lose me again.

"Where are you taking us exactly?" Easter asked and I snapped back to the moment.

"Medical level," Mario said. "We snagged a few off a transport truck but they were pretty roughed up. We've got them sedated, but there is one giving us a real problem. Every time we try to bring him out, he about loses his mind. And if he blows his top, it'll bring every monster down on us."

Easter shook her head. "Seems stupid to keep him then."

He looked over his shoulder, past her to me. "Ah, I don't think my sister would like me much if I killed him. He's shockingly handsome."

Dinah sucked in a sharp breath and I was running before I could think better of it. There was no pretending in this, not for me.

"Take the next left!" Mario called after me as I hit the T intersection. I bounced off the far wall, pushing off with my feet and then pounded down the hall to the double doors at the end. I burst through them to see six beds, three occupied. Catching my entrance, a couple healers cringed back.

He was in the last bed on the right and I strode toward him. Seeing him, truly seeing him. He wasn't dead. He wasn't in a facility.

His face was bruised, and he had a jagged cut on his forehead that would leave a scar, for sure. Across his chest, I could see where the bruises on his ribs were fading, where his body was slowly healing. But none of that mattered. He was alive.

Hands and feet were strapped down tightly at the wrists and ankles, and a blanket was thrown over his lower body. His chest was bare and his skin was dimpled with goose flesh in the cool air, the pulse of his heart beating in the hollow of his throat.

My hand hovered for a moment before I let it slowly drop and rest over his heart.

"Killian."

ALSO BY SHANNON MAYER

The Forty Proof Series

MIDLIFE BOUNTY HUNTER

MIDLIFE FAIRY HUNTER

MIDLIFE DEMON HUNTER

MIDLIFE GHOST HUNTER

MIDLIFE ZOMBIE HUNTER

MIDLIFE WITCH HUNTER

MIDLIFE MAGIC HUNTER

MIDLIFE SOUL HUNTER

The Honey and Ice Series (with Kelly St. Clare)

A COURT OF HONEY AND ASH

A THRONE OF FEATHERS AND BONE

A CROWN OF PETALS AND ICE

World of Honey and Ice (with Kelly St. Clare)

THORN KISSED & SILVER CHAINS

IVY TOUCHED & BRONZE BLADE

Rylee Adamson Series

TRACKING MAGIC (short)

ELEMENTALLY PRICELESS (novella)

ALEX (short)

PRICELESS

IMMUNE

RAISING INNOCENCE

SHADOWED THREADS

BLIND SALVAGE

TRACKER

GUARDIAN (novella)

VEILED THREAT

WOUNDED

STITCHED (novella)

RISING DARKNESS

BLOOD OF THE LOST

Rylee Adamson Epilogues

RYLEE

LIAM

PAMELA

LYNCHPIN

The Elemental Series

RECURVE

BREAKWATER

FIRESTORM

WINDBURN

ROOTBOUND

ASH

DESTROYER

Questing Witch Series

AIMLESS WITCH

CARAVAN WITCH

MAZE WITCH

ELEMENTAL WITCH

The Nix Series

FURY OF A PHOENIX

BLOOD OF A PHOENIX

RISE OF A PHOENIX

A SAVAGE SPELL

A KILLING CURSE

The Golden Wolf

GOLDEN

GLITTER

GOSSAMER

The Alpha Territories

TAKEN BY FATE

HUNTED BY FATE

CLAIMED BY FATE

FOR A COMPLETE BOOK LIST VISIT

www.shannonmayer.com

A KILLING CURSE

CHAPTER 1

PHOENIX

Killian was alive. The heart beating under my hand was steady and strong, even if the man it belonged to seemed to be in some sort of coma. The world around me slid away for a few minutes as I stared down at him. As I let my fingers thread through his hair and trace the lines of his face.

I touched one of his hands—there were burns that traced like lightning up from his fingertips to his elbow and even further, the lines reached up to his shoulder. If I stared long enough, they looked like they were moving, as if the marks were alive and trying to swallow him whole.

The threat of Gardreel and the fallen, the threat of the handlers and the institutions, the threat of being tracked or even the threat of the people around me, abnormals I barely knew—all of it was gone in those few moments.

Easter slid a chair over to me and I sat, without a word, and without taking my hand off Killian's chest. Because a very small part of me feared that if I stopped touching him, he'd disappear. Like before.

Like my entire world before. For the moment, keeping my hands on him meant we would be okay. That he would live. Though I could see that death was stalking him closely.

"I'll get us some food." Easter didn't touch me, but I could feel her energy, like she wanted to. "We both need to eat."

I nodded, not trusting myself to speak for fear of what might come out. Screams? Maybe. Sobs? No, none of those. But I might start yelling at Killian. I might start killing those around me out of sheer frustration.

"You better not die on me," I said quietly to him. I wanted to see his lips turn upward, wanted to see him open his eyes and tell me he'd just been waiting for me to show. He did neither.

All I could do was just sit there and breathe him in. It had been over a year that we'd been apart, over a year since I knew for sure if he was alive, if I knew that he was with my children, protecting them. Children, not child.

We'd had a daughter, a girl who'd survived when I'd been told she'd not. A pain I did not like, because I'd lived it before, cut through me. When I'd thought Bear had been dead, there had been nothing left in me. Nothing but the need to kill those who'd taken my child from me.

A shuddering breath caught me off guard and I finally found my voice. "Did you name her, Killian?"

Not that I expected him to answer, not really.

He was calm under my hand, but there was a stillness to him that I didn't like, that I didn't understand. As an abnormal he healed faster than a human, and as a powerful abnormal he should have been awake by now. Even I could see the injuries he'd taken were mostly gone. I brushed my fingers over the angry red lines that ran across his chest, neck and arms. Almost like the electricity he had control over had come back to bite him.

Or had he been lashed? I let my fingers do the work and closed my eyes. No, these wounds were something else; they weren't from a leather lash, and they weren't from knives. They pulsed under my fingertips.

"The wings did it."

I opened my eyes and turned to see Mario standing ten feet back and leaning against the wall.

"The wings," I said.

"That's what he was ranting when we brought

him in. Whatever it was he'd been fighting had cut him up with their wings. We assumed it was some kind of abnormal that was working with the labs. Maybe some sort of shifter."

I pressed harder against the scars, and they . . . pushed back. Yes, something was in there. "How long did it take to heal over the wounds?"

"Not long, a few hours." Mario shrugged but didn't come closer. His eyes were like mine, dark and wary. He had every reason to fear me. And I had every reason not to trust him.

I frowned as I felt the edges of the scars. It was more like his skin had been torn open than properly cut. Maybe like a rough-edged stone knife. Keeping my hand against the one scar, I let my fingers walk the length of it.

"He's been talking in his sleep—if you'd call this sleep—and muttering names. Someone named Bear?" Mario offered those words, and I did not react. Couldn't.

"Anything else?"

"Angel. That's the only other name that he's given. The rest is just the usual, what you'd expect of someone who has been fighting his whole life, telling us to fuck off, telling us he'll kill us." Mario pushed off the wall and slowly made his way over to the other side of Killian. "He won't last long under this spell, curse, or whatever it is. Days at best. We can get fluid into him, but not much. Not enough, and we don't have even an IV bag to our name here."

Mario was not wrong. Even in the short time that I'd been sitting with him, Killian's heartrate had slowed—fractionally, but I'd felt it. His skin had cooled too—the same as his heart, it was fractional but with time it would slide into icy cold. He'd be dead soon if I did nothing.

"What are you suggesting?"

"That you put him out of his misery," Mario said. "When the time comes."

I had Dinah out and pointed at my brother before he could so much as blink. "I think you should keep your mercy killing ideas to yourself, Mario."

Ruby, the Cane Corso-pitbull cross that had chosen me as her person, let out a low growl at my side, pressing her body to my thigh as she picked up on my anger. That rumbling growl was wet and throaty and she took a step toward him. Mario gave her a long look, his eyes a little wider.

Dinah gave a low snort. "Lesson one. She doesn't give up on people. Lesson two, piss her off and find out how short her fuse is. I dare you. I'd have no problem shooting you."

From my back, Diego chuckled. "And if the ladies won't, I'll happily blow a hole in your middle."

Mario shrugged, reached out and pushed Dinah to the side.

Wrong move.

I was up and on him, driving him to the ground and jamming Dinah under his chin in one single move, my finger hovering over the trigger. "Never touch my gun without permission."

Ruby was at my side and her teeth were bared, inches from his face. As if Dinah wasn't enough of a threat.

Diego whispered, "Please, please let me kill him."

Dinah just laughed. "Oh, he fucked up already. Tell him to put his finger in me, I'd like that. Then I'll blow his whole fucking hand off."

Mario locked eyes with me. "You would kill me for touching your gun. Are you serious?"

"I would kill you for not understanding that I don't have the bandwidth for other people's bullshit right now." I got off him and stepped back, and tucked Dinah into her holster. "But I won't because our numbers are down. And we need every mother-fucking abnormal we can get. Especially those who have some leadership qualities."

I stepped back from him, keeping him in my sights. He stood and brushed his clothes off, keeping an eye on Ruby, but otherwise acting for all the world like nothing had just happened. "I always thought the rumors about you were . . . elaborated. I stand corrected." He gave me a tight nod. "When you're ready to discuss the next step—"

"Ten minutes," I said. Because if I let myself stay and keep on touching Killian, I wouldn't be able to leave him. And right then we had things that needed discussing. "Give me ten minutes and then I will talk to you about our next steps."

Discussing things like how to stop the fallen.

Mario looked at Killian. "You don't have much time with him."

He wasn't telling me anything I didn't already know. Killian was dying, right in front of me, and there was very little I could do. I shook my head. "He won't die today. Let's get shit handled. Give me ten minutes."

My brother's eyes narrowed, thoughtful, and then he gave me that same nod as before. "I'll wait for you."

He left me there and I sat back down, letting my fingers once more trace across Killian's body.

Wings did this, like the wings of the leather-clad, multi-armed fallen that had attacked us at Carlos's house. I pulled one of my knives out of my boot sheath, and laid the razor-sharp tip against one of the scars. Not like another scar would bother Killian any. And I needed to see what was underneath. What was pulsing against my fingers.

Pressing down, I slid it into the flesh, opening the wound.

The smell was first putrid, like decomposing

meat. The deep green pus, streaked through with black and red, was next, oozing out and down his side. "Fuck, Dinah, you see this?" Tiny chunks of what looked like leather burbled out too. Bits of wing?

"Jesus, that's bad. You're going to have to lance them all."

Diego let out a hiss. "You need some antiseptic. And wash your hands before you touch me again. That's gross."

I went to work, cutting open every ridged scar across Killian's chest, belly and upper arms. All of them were completely infected. Two I had to cut deeper and put pressure on in order to get the thick pus out, to literally pop them open and force the chunks to go. Those two were darker than the others, the pus nearly solid black.

Those two had something else in them. Something sharp and hard. I touched the foreign object with the tip of my knife.

Killian let out a low groan as he lifted a hand as if he'd stop me.

"Sorry, you have no choice in this." I leaned over his chest, my fingers and knife working in tandem to pull the objects out of him. They were stuck hard and I ended up with a knee on his side and pulling with all my weight before they let go.

Stumbling back, I held the shiny black piece of

wing in my hand. The scales were the same as those on the ones I'd fought. I lay them in my hand and bounced them there.

Killian had damaged the fallen, broken off parts of them, and those parts had sunk into him. And even as I looked at them . . . they dissolved in my hands. Ruby snuffled at the dust, blowing it around the room. She gave a snort and then looked up at me with her one eye.

As if she wasn't sure. "Bad guys," I said. "This is what the bad guys smell like."

She woofed as if she understood.

I drew in a long slow breath as I considered the situation. The dust that was on my palms, and on the floor, was all that was left of the fallen. Something Killian had done had killed or injured them, and something in his blood had finished them off.

The only question was . . . what?

CHAPTER 2

Ruby snuffled around the floor, licking up the ashes of the fallen. I didn't stop her; I doubted it would hurt her at all. And maybe she'd get a taste for the fuckers. I rubbed my fingers together. The ashes were not greasy at all—not the way I'd expect them to be.

I dusted my hands on my pants, but the shit stuck to me, like glitter. "Fucking angel glitter," I muttered.

And then I froze. "Dinah."

"Yeah?"

I dropped to the floor as I spoke, scooping up the glitter. "Think you could shove this angel dust shit into a couple of bullets?"

I scooped the dust into a small pile, pinched a bit, then put it down her barrel. The thing about the sentient guns was they could from time to time use an outside ingredient. But it was touch and go.

Everyone kept saying that the fallen's abilities were the only thing that could kill another fallen.

But what about some of their ashes?

"Shit, that's a fucking brilliant idea!" She trembled in my hand as I scooped all the dust down her barrel. "You must get your brains from your sister."

"Sure didn't get them from my dad," I muttered.

She laughed. I laughed. We loaded her up to hopefully be able to do some damage.

Her inner workings clicked and rumbled as I held her. "What do you think?" I asked.

"I've managed to meld it with my explosive rounds. I think that was best." She made a clicking noise that made me think of someone licking their lips. "Three shots. Not enough, but that could mean all the difference."

"That's what I'm hoping."

I stood and looked back to Killian. He hadn't moved—again, not that I expected him to jump up and down just from having his wounds lanced.

He did, however, open his eyes a crack. "Lass?"

I moved to his side and took his hand. "Killian?"

"Dying," he whispered. "Kids safe."

I wasn't sure if he was asking or telling me. "For now, yes. They are."

His eyes closed and that smile I loved slid over his lips, but not another word. His hand went limp in mine as he fell back under whatever held him in thrall.

"We have to hurry," Dinah said. "That man is too fine to just let him die on a table."

"Is he really?" Diego grumbled. "I mean, I am a very fine man. People just let me die."

"Oh, shut up with you," Dinah snapped. The two of them set to bickering as I took a cloth from the table next to Killian, poured some rubbing alcohol on it, and wiped his wounds down. They had already closed, but the alcohol helped with the stench.

If he didn't come out of this coma soon, I would lance them again.

"Why would he get an infection?" Diego asked. "Abnormals don't generally get hurt like that."

I motioned to his hands. "Looks like he encountered the same shit that Cowboy touched. The angel dust they use to knock abnormals out."

The implication was clear, at least to me.

Cowboy had enough demon in him to freak out Ornias, and that was the reason why he'd reacted so badly. That had to be the reason why they both reacted to the dust this way. Not because they were abnormal, but because they both had a good amount of demon blood in them.

It was as good a guess as any, not that it changed how I felt about him. If he was a demon, then he was my demon.

I leaned over and pressed my lips to his. They were a little warmer. Or maybe that was hope giving me a false lead. "Don't die, Killian."

I left him there and stepped out of the room. Mario didn't ask what I'd done, though I saw his nose curl on the scent that had clung to me. I wiped the knife on the cloth and then tossed that in a nearby cannister. "Infection, I lanced it. That will give us time to figure out how to help him."

He nodded. "You're ready to plan then?"

I waved at him. "Lead the way."

"Of course." Mario turned his back to me, giving me a perfect shot if I'd wanted to kill him without a fuss.

Dinah let out an exasperated sigh, but she kept her voice low and just for me and Diego. "How is it that he doesn't know you? He was around when we were hunting abnormals. Look at this, so fucking trusting!"

"She was out of the circuit a long time," Diego rumbled from my back. "She has become myth and legend and those that never really dealt with her before don't believe that she is who the stories say."

Technically Mario *had* been around when I'd worked for my father, but he'd been small potatoes. And he'd stayed clear of the big players. Which made more sense now that I knew he was my father's son. My brother.

If I was being honest, he'd been smarter than the rest of us, staying far away from the family and the horrors that the rest of us had lived through.

"What is your plan for everyone here?" I asked.

He looked over his shoulder. "To keep them alive."

"Other than the obvious."

He gave me an odd look and I smiled, understanding clearly that he didn't want to talk.

"Dinah," I said as Mario led me through the old factory, "it looks like he doesn't want to talk where his own people can hear him. Which means he has secrets he doesn't want them to know."

She shivered. "Oh, I love secrets. How about you, Diego? You like a good secret?"

"Only if it's really juicy."

I watched Mario's back, noticed the tightening across his shoulders. The tension growing.

"You think that they know he doesn't trust them?" I asked loud enough that my voice echoed through the space we were in. A long hall, one of a few that we'd walked.

Diego and Dinah laughed together, as if we'd practiced this moment. "No, they don't know he'd throw them to the fallen if it was his life or theirs," Diego said. "A man after my own heart."

Mario swung around, his one hand coming up,

light with a dark red fire. "I suggest you and your friends shut your mouths."

He wanted to play with fire, did he?

I stepped up and put my hand over his, dousing his flames. "Don't make that mistake, Mario. I want to like you. But the fact is you don't trust your people. That does not bode well." I pushed my hand into his and called up my own fire, dragging it through me and pushing it to my hand.

The bright yellow fire was edged with white licks, brighter than the last time I'd used it. Far brighter. He winced and pulled his hand away.

"I don't need them knowing that there are moles." He ground the words out. "I am looking for them. But I have to be sure. As you said, we need all the people we can pull together."

For a fight? I frowned at him and pulled my hand away. "You think it will come to a battle?"

He closed his eyes and tipped his head back. "Can you just fucking wait until we get to my office?"

Dinah laughed. "We're on a bit of a time crunch, right? You know that?"

His eyes shot to my holster. "What is her name?"

"Dinah," she barked. "And that big bastard on her back is Diego. Kind of shit aim on him, but with a big barrel, who cares if the aim is any good, am I right?"

Mario's eyebrows shot up. "What do you mean there is a time crunch?"

"Just a feeling," Dinah said. "I have those."

He sighed. "We are almost to my office. Can you just give it a minute?"

I motioned for him to go with a wave of my hand.

As we walked I couldn't help but notice the warren of halls and doors, many that were obviously created in recent months by the shiny welds and the shit material. The factory was a maze that would give them an edge if Gardreel and his fallen were to drop in unannounced.

We intersected with Easter on the main floor. She had two plates of food and a look of irritation written clearly on her face. Ruby gave a woof, greeting her. I took one of the plates of food and she silently stepped in beside me.

"I got turned around in here," she said. "This place . . . there is Hider magic in it, but something else too."

"A spell to keep it not only hidden, but twisted," Mario said. "We have a few spell casters, they have been working nonstop to keep us safe."

"There will be a cost to that," Easter said. "Spells always have a kickback. You know that."

"I do." Mario nodded at her, his eyes drifting over her face.

Dinah gave a low whistle. "Several spell casters working at once? That's a big kickback."

Interesting that Dinah had a thought about spell casting. Then again, she'd been stuffed into a gun with a spell.

The factory was quiet with the exception of our voices, but I could sense abnormals watching us. My skin was crawling by the time we'd climbed a final two sets of stairs to a large open office space that looked out over the factory floor. Ruby kept pace, her toes clicking on the hard surface, her hackles rising as we went, her one good eye watching all around us.

I didn't blame her, especially when we got to the top of the stairs.

The metal door with the heavy hinges gave me pause, the bands of iron on it meant to keep people out. Or people in, depending on how you looked at it.

Carlos and Pete already waited for us inside the room, Carlos with a coffee mug wrapped up in his hands. Pete sat with his eyes closed as if he were sleeping, leaned back in his chair. But I could see the pulse in his neck and the flare in his nostrils that said he was faking it. He'd already smelled us coming, or at the very least me and the rot that was all over my hands.

"Was it really him?" Carlos asked as Mario stepped into the room.

I nodded. "Yes." My feet stopped at the threshold of the door, as did Easter. Mario was inside the room, and already sitting in a chair behind a large desk. He looked over his shoulder. "What is wrong?"

I rapped my knuckles on the metal. "What the fuck is this two-ton metal door for?"

Mario made a sweeping gesture with his hands, encompassing the factory. "There are a number of abnormals with exceptional hearing. This room is soundproof even to them. As I was trying to get you to see," he lowered his voice. "There are those who might not be fully in our camp."

Sure, that made sense. But I didn't want to go into a locked room like this. Call it PTSD, but the idea of shutting a massive metal door behind me, hearing it click shut . . . it made me want to kill people.

"I don't trust anyone, dear sister." He smiled, a genuine one as far as I could see. "Not even you. Especially not your dog. I think she'd like to eat me."

Outwardly, I kept my face calm. Hell, I even smiled, though I knew the coldness of my visage. "Best not to trust family. In my experience, they'll screw you over every chance they can get."

"Amen," Easter said. "My own mother sold me to the highest bidder."

"Double that," Dinah grumbled. "Look at me, I got screwed by the man who said he'd love me forever."

"Men are the worst." Easter nodded. "Especially the ones who lie."

Dinah snickered. "You mean all of them?"

They laughed, I did not. Because I knew that it was an easy shot at men, when they didn't all lie. There were a few good ones left. Like Killian.

I blinked, shocked at my thoughts. Fuck, I was going soft.

"I'll give you the key if that makes you feel better?" Mario offered, though there was a tone to his voice that was pure condescension. "But we cannot have this conversation where others can hear us. Unless you want to risk information getting back to the fallen ones?"

Even as he spoke, the sensation of being watched intensified. Motherfucker Gardreel had people everywhere. We needed time, and I would make that time happen.

"You know what? Hold that thought while I do your work for you." I put my plate of food on the floor, turned and strode down the stairs, snapping my fingers for Ruby to follow me.

She trotted down next to me and then sat at my side as I did a visual sweep of the space around us. "Find the bad guys, Ruby."

Not exactly the same training that Abe had, but in her own way she was more tightly bound to me. I'd told her that the dust she'd sniffed up had been the bad guys. Her one eye drooped shut and she sniffed the air, then put her nose to the ground.

She did a circle around me, wider and wider.

"I thought you said we were on a time crunch?" Mario barked.

"I thought you said you had moles," I snapped back. "And since you can't find them, and dig them the fuck out, I will!"

Maybe I was in a bad mood. Maybe I just wanted to kill something. Both were plausible.

As it was. Someone was going to die. It was just a matter of who.

Keep reading
A KILLING CURSE
The Nix Series Book 5

Made in the USA
Middletown, DE
08 November 2024